Resort
to
Murder

D1311114

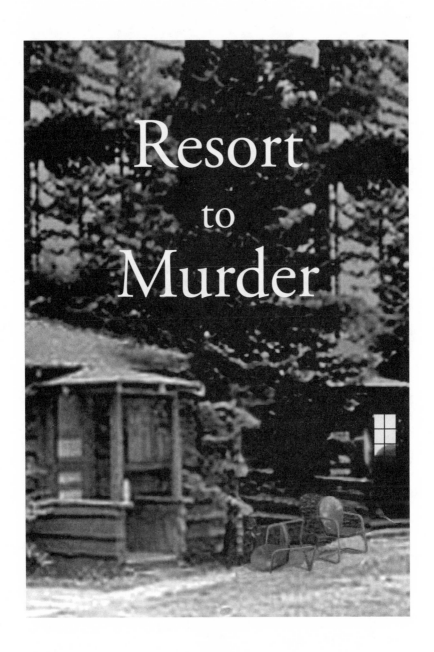

Resort
to
Murder

NODIN PRESS

Our special thanks to: Jean Brookins, Lorna Landvik, Norton Stillman, John Toren, all the writers who submitted stories we couldn't include, and readers of mystery fiction everywhere.

ISBN 10: 1-932472-47-9
ISBN 13: 978-1-932472-47-9
Library of Congress Control Number: 2007930596
Cover and layout: John Toren

Nodin Press, LLC
530 N. Third Street, Suite 120
Minneapolis, MN 55401

TABLE OF CONTENTS

Introduction

Lorna Landvik

Minnesota has over 10,000 lakes and there's something in the water. Some enzyme, some undiscovered microbe that seeps its way into the psyches of normal, everyday people and turns them into…mystery writers.

Or are they the ones at the lutefisk buffet, helping themselves to seconds because they know preserved-in-lye cod sparks something in the brain? Or are they able to translate messages from the pulsations of the northern lights?

Something's got to explain why Minnesota has bred so many mystery writers—so many good mystery writers.

A novelist myself, I am often asked if I will ever write crime fiction but in response, I can only shake my head and admit defeat.

"You'd know who did it by page two."

I'm not that kind of weaver, able to thread plot lines and pace and characters, real clues and red herrings into the richly-textured and deeply-colored fabric that is a good mystery.

But if they're not inspired by enchanted waters or putrid fish or watching the skies, what makes a writer write mystery? Life is a puzzle; is it their desire to create a world in which they get to figure things out? To solve problems? Or like a mischievous park ranger, do they get pleasure from pointing out the swooping hawks in the sky, only to reprimand us for not paying attention to the bear up the path? I do think humor—a sly sense of humor—is a common trait in mystery writers; they like to mess with us. And the best ones create characters we care about, characters whose fates matter, who when imperiled make us gasp and shout, "Watch out!"

Maybe when you read this collection, you'll be 'up at the cabin,' or at an ice rink, reading between periods of your daughter's hockey game, or hunkered down in a back booth of a diner with good pie and a waitress who refills your coffee cup without your asking. But even if you're not in a place classically Minnesotan, your enjoyment won't be diminished. These stories will take you there; transportation provided by some of the best of Minnesota's mystery writers.

And if one day a biochemist discovers that yes, the properties of lutefisk, when ingested by certain susceptible people, can inspire them to create compelling mysteries, well, you read it here first.

– Lorna Landvik

Resort

to

Murder

William Kent Krueger

Raised in the Cascade Mountains of Oregon, William Kent Krueger briefly attended Stanford University—before being kicked out for radical activities. After that, he logged timber, worked construction, tried his hand at free-lance journalism, and eventually ended up researching child development at the University of Minnesota. He currently earns his living as a full-time author. He's been married for 35 years to a marvelous woman who is an attorney. He makes his home in St. Paul, a city he dearly loves.

Krueger writes the Cork O'Connor mystery series set in the great north woods of Minnesota, hard up against the Iron Range. His work has received many awards, including the Minnesota Book Award, the Loft-McKnight Fiction Award, and the Anthony Award for Best Novel in both 2005 and 2006, for Blood Hollow *and* Mercy Falls, *respectively. In 2007* Copper River *won the Minnesota Book Award for Genre Fiction.*

Hills Like White Rabbits

William Kent Krueger

Cooper knew they planned to kill him. Exactly how was the part that was still a mystery.

All the way to Duluth, there'd been snow. As soon as he and Charlotte passed Spirit Mountain, the weather cleared miraculously, and the hills ahead were like frightened white rabbits hunched against the painful blue of the winter sky.

"Tell me you love me," Cooper said.

"You know I do."

"Tell me," he said.

She didn't reply, only stared at Lake Superior, a vast frozen sea that, at the eastern horizon, cut off the sky as cleanly as the cold blade of an ax.

He should have known from the beginning they were doomed. She was, after all, thirty years younger than he and terribly beautiful. He'd hired her to help with his research on a book for which he'd received a healthy seven-figure advance. For too long now he'd wrestled hopelessly with that manuscript. In the meantime he'd married Charlotte. When he was a younger man, words and women had been his servants. Now they only betrayed him.

"You can't say it, can you?" he pressed her.

She looked at him. Her eyes were gray, like old snow.

"I love you," she said.

They drove up Highway 1 to Ely then north to the very edge of the Boundary Waters Canoe Area Wilderness. The roads ran through corridors of plowed snow. The rugged hills were thick with pines. Beneath the trees everything was bone white.

Camp L'Etoile du Nord sat on a far northern arm of the lake. It was run by one of those charitable organizations that believe in the inherent goodness of people, something Cooper did not. But he liked the place. He'd come here as a boy with his family, spent long weeks canoeing and swimming in summer, cross-country skiing and snowshoeing in winter. Shortly after Christmas, as their second anniversary approached, Charlotte complained that even the big house on Crocus Hill had become too constricting. They needed to get away from St. Paul, she declared, or she'd go crazy. His writing had made him rich and he could have stayed anywhere. It was, he fully realized, a pathetically sentimental connection with a happier past that made him choose Camp L'Etoile.

The day before they left, in the late afternoon when she thought he was napping, he overheard her part of a cell phone conversation in the atrium.

"Don't worry," Charlotte had said. "He's so absorbed with himself he doesn't notice anything. He has no idea."

Her back was to Cooper. The winter sunlight came at her almost horizontally through the long windows and her skin looked as if she'd powdered herself with saffron.

"Tell me again how you'll do it," Charlotte said. She listened. There was a little chuckle in her throat. "He'll never know what hit him." She put her hand to the window and left a small moist palm print on the glass. "We'll be there tomorrow. I'll do my part, you do yours, Jack. When it's all over, we'll have each other again."

He retreated and waited.

Jack?

He realized he knew dismally little about his wife. He made a noise in the hallway and entered the atrium. She turned to him and smiled, innocent as a baby scorpion.

There were cabins of various sizes at the camp. Cooper had reserved a small unit that sat on a rocky promontory above the flat frozen lake. When they were settled in, he suggested they go cross-country skiing.

"You go," she said. "I'm a little tired."

By myself? he wondered. *Or will Jack be waiting somewhere along the trail?*

In his early years as a journalist, Cooper had covered the Vietnam War. He'd worn a helmet and a flak jacket, carried a Colt Python on his hip. In an ambush in Phuoc Long Province, he'd

fought with the grunts whose story he was writing. He'd killed a
Viet Cong soldier that day. He wrote the story for the *New Yorker*
and it was made into a movie. Later he wrote a book, a novel of
his experience. It was, in truth, more fiction than fact, but it won
him a Pulitzer and gave him a certain reputation that he liked and
cultivated. Over the years he'd repeated so often the stories he'd
created about himself that he'd come to believe them. He wasn't
particularly worried about meeting this Jack fellow on the trail.

"I'll start dinner," Charlotte said. "It'll be here nice and hot
when you come back."

"Of course it will," Cooper said.

The idea of what might be waiting for him in the woods was
oddly exciting, and when he kissed her goodbye, he kissed her pas-
sionately. He slapped her butt playfully on the way out.

"After dinner," he said, "we'll do dessert."

He followed a trail that took him to the edge of the Boundary
Waters. The sun sat low in the sky and he skied through the haunt-
ing blue shadow of hills. The air was like ice pressed against his skin.
The only sounds were his heavy breathing and the sizzle of his skis
over snow. He scanned the woods constantly. In a way, it was like
being back in Nam. The tension was exhilarating, and the constant
bump of the powerful little .32 Beretta he'd slipped into his parka
pocket was reassuring.

He returned just after sunset, stepped off his skis, and leaned
them against the outside wall of the cabin. When he entered, he
found a fire roaring in the fireplace and Charlotte with another
man.

"This is John Ashton," Charlotte said. "He wanted to meet
you."

Ashton rose from the table where he'd been sitting with Cooper's wife, drinking a glass of red wine. He thrust out his hand.

"I hope you don't mind me being so forward," Ashton said.
"When I found out you'd be here, I had to meet you. I'm a huge
fan of your work."

"That so?" Cooper said.

He took the man's hand. Ashton was tall, willowy, good looking. Cooper pegged him at not much older than Charlotte.

"I did my master's thesis on your Vietnam book."

"You're not the first," Cooper said.

"I'm sure." Ashton smiled. His teeth were ridiculously white.

"John, eh? Go by Jack?"

"Not usually," Ashton said.

Right, Cooper thought.

"Why don't you join us for dinner?" Cooper offered.

"Thanks, but I don't want to intrude. I've got stew on the stove in my own cabin. Then I've got a reservation for the sauna at eight. But I'm here for several days, so I'm sure we'll be running into each other."

"I'm sure," Cooper said.

Ashton, in parting, took Charlotte's hand. When Cooper saw the desire in the man's eyes, a cold satisfaction settled on his heart.

They'd been happy once. Cooper remembered how, in the beginning, Charlotte would lean over his shoulder, pointing out something among the documents on Cooper's desk. She was excited to be helping him, honored, she'd said. It wasn't her adulation that captured him. Adulation he'd had in spades. It was that she was genuine. Her face gave away everything about her, and when Cooper saw in that beautiful face that she loved him, he was genuinely touched. He could be difficult. "Irascible" was among the kinder adjectives often applied to him. But Charlotte seemed to look beyond the unpleasant exterior and saw something in him that was still worth loving. He married her with a full heart.

It was his fault that things had gone so bad; he was man enough to own that. Still, you can't love a dragon and not expect to get burned now and then. When he burned her with his caustic tongue, she showed her hurt. That was another part of being genuine. Whenever he knew he'd hurt her, instead of saying he was sorry, he blamed her for her tears, blamed her damned thin skin, blamed her for loving him. After he overheard the conversation in the atrium and thought about it, he wasn't really surprised. He probably had it coming. What surprised him was that he hadn't been able to see it sooner, to see in that beautiful, open face the desperation he'd driven her to.

That night Cooper got drunk, rip-snorting drunk. Charlotte sat by the fire she'd built and hugged herself as if, despite the leaping flames, she was cold.

"Frigid," he accused when she refused his advances.

"Why do you get so mean?" she asked. "Is it the book?"

"Screw the bloody book. Let's go for a walk."

"I'd rather not."

"Fine. I'll go alone. Maybe I'll bump into Jack."

"Jack?"

"Our friend Ashton."

"Please don't go," she said, looking a little panicked. "You're drunk and it's dangerously cold outside. Just stay."

He stood at the door, considering her concern. Was it for him or Jack?

He blew her a kiss. "I'll come to thee by moonlight though hell should bar the way," he said and left.

There was no moon, but the snow grabbed the ambient light of the stars and threw it before Cooper so that he could see quite well. He made his way along the path to the sauna, a large log structure built at the very edge of the lake. Because a lot of people went naked when they used the sauna, you were supposed to make a reservation, as Ashton had. When he stepped into the outer changing room, he could feel the powerful heat from the stove on the other side of the inner wall. It was not quite eight o'clock. The sauna was empty.

A sign on the door declared prominently: USE CAUTION ON THE RAMP TO THE LAKE. IT MAY BE ICY.

The sign referred to the ramp that ran from the sauna down to the frozen lake. You could, if you so desired, finish your sauna experience with a dip in the frigid lake water, done by plunging through a hole that was kept open in the ice.

He stepped into the building and shed his clothing. He folded the items and set them on the bottom bench. He left his socks on, a trick he'd learned years before when he visited Camp L'Etoile. When you ran down to the lake, the socks kept your skin from freezing to the ramp and helped keep you from slipping on the ice. Cooper stepped into the hot blast of the sauna room. The room was lined with cedar. Three tiers of wooden benches mounted the far wall. He dipped water from the bucket beside the door and splashed the hot rocks of the stove. Steam shot upward in a long hiss.

The Finns, when they came to the North Country, built saunas before they put up any other structure. A sensible people, Cooper thought, as he climbed to the top tier and settled back.

He'd had two wives before Charlotte. Through his drinking, his philandering, his struggle to be the image he'd created of himself, he'd driven them both away. Although he had more acquaintances than he could remember, he'd been desperately lonely until Charlotte. Now not only had he pushed her away, he'd driven her to a desperate act. He didn't blame her. He was a bastard, a bona fide son of a bitch.

Maybe it was the heat that loosened him, or the alcohol, or the exhaustion from the long drive and the skiing, but suddenly he found himself crying like a damn baby.

The sauna door opened and Ashton stepped in, naked. He saw Cooper and looked startled. "Sorry," he said. "I thought I had this hour."

Cooper wiped at the tears that mixed with the salt of the sweat running down his face. He said, "Join me," as if the hour were his to offer.

Ashton seemed disconcerted, but he finally shrugged and joined Cooper on the top bench. For a while, the two men sat, silent and naked in a room hot as hell.

"You like my work," Cooper said.

"You're a great stylist," Ashton replied.

"Stylist? What about the meat of the stories?"

Ashton was quiet on that point. Finally he said, "I don't always agree with your take on life."

"No? What's your take on life, Jack?"

"It's John."

"Whatever."

"I don't always agree with what you seem to see as a definition of manhood."

"You ever kill a man?" Cooper said.

"I can't say that I have."

"Been in a desperate fight, *mano-a-mano*?"

"Not really."

"Then what the hell do you know about being a man?"

"I'd say a man is a lot more than a trigger finger or a pair of fists."

Cooper laughed. "You know what it all boils down to, boy?

This: Do you have the balls to do what needs to be done?"

"There are other ways to deal with life. It doesn't always have to be about conflict."

"A coward's rationale."

"All right," Ashton said, turning to him, "since you've opened the door. One of the criticisms I leveled at your work in my thesis is that your view of life is naively simplistic. Man is *this*, woman is *this*, the world is *this*. You're like an artist with one color on his palette. The triumph of your writing is that within the context of the story, you make that view acceptable, believable even. In the real world, however, it's bunk. Forgive me for speaking plainly."

"Forgive you for talking like a man? Don't be ridiculous. Forgive you for reducing the sum of my work to a flat cliché about some goddamn painter, now that's something else."

"I didn't mean it that way."

"Backing away from a fight already? And this one's only literary. You've got a lot to learn about being a man, Jack."

"Look, maybe I'd best just leave the sauna to you."

"Are you married?"

Ashton had started to rise. The question made him pause. He sat back down.

"No," he said.

"Ever?"

"No."

"You're not gay are you?"

"No. Not that it's any business of yours."

"Girlfriend? Significant relationship?"

Ashton had jet black hair, a lot of it. It hung down his forehead and sweat followed it, channeling into his eyes. He wiped his face with the back of his right arm. "Yes," he answered. "But it's rather...complicated."

"What's complicated about it?"

"There's an obstacle."

"Hell, remove it."

"It's not that easy."

"What's so hard? Me, I killed a man once," Cooper said.

"I know. Everybody knows. That was a long time ago, Mr.

Cooper. And under extraordinary circumstances."

"You know anything about cannibalism?"

"Not to speak of."

"People who've done it say it's amazing. Liberating. Exhilarating." Cooper leaned toward Ashton, as if to confide. "I didn't just kill the man, Jack. I fed on him."

Ashton looked as if he was sure Cooper was crazy.

"I don't mean literally. I didn't eat his flesh. I mean I fed on the experience of killing him."

Ashton said, "In your books, you often compare killing to sex. Now you're saying it's like cannibalism? This is all a stretch."

"Unless you've been there you wouldn't know, would you?"

Cooper was dripping gallons of sweat himself. His skin felt as hot as the rocks on the stove. His head was filled with a roaring as from a great fire.

"Being a man comes down to one simple question, Jack: What kind of *cojones* do you have?"

He stared at Ashton until the man looked away.

"Let me show you something," Cooper said. He made his way down from the bench and motioned Ashton to follow. He shoved open the door to the ramp that led to the lake. "Out here," he said.

Against the side of the sauna was stacked the wood that was used to stoke the stove inside. Cooper picked up a thick length of hardwood—maple, he thought. When Ashton came through the door, Cooper swung it and caught the man in the back of the head. Ashton went down. Cooper hit him one more time for good measure. He dragged Ashton onto the ramp that was icy from the water earlier sauna-users had dripped on their way to and from the open hole in the frozen lake. He arranged Ashton so that it appeared the man had slipped, fallen, and hit the back of his head. A tendril of blood crept from Ashton's wet black hair and tinted the ice. The thermometer that hung on the side of the sauna indicated the air temperature was twelve degrees above zero. If Ashton was not dead yet, in a few minutes the cold would finish the job. Cooper removed Ashton's socks and put them with the rest of the man's clothing. Finally he took the piece of maple he'd used, threw it in the stove in the sauna, and watched the evidence of his crime begin to burn to ash.

That's the way a man takes care of things, he thought with more satisfaction than he'd felt about anything in years.

As he walked back to the cabin, he considered what he would tell Charlotte. That on his walk he'd stood under the stars and realized that, like one of those beauties of the night sky, she sparkled brightly in his life. He would promise that from now on things would be different. And they would be. They would be.

Ashton was wrong, he thought. Life was that simple.

He opened the door and there it sat propped on a chair: a portrait of them together, he and Charlotte, done in oil and showing them in a happier time. They stood in the garden of the house on Crocus Hill and everything around them was in bloom.

"Happy anniversary," Charlotte said.

Christ, he'd been thinking about this other thing and he'd forgotten.

Charlotte smiled at the astonishment on his face. "I had a friend of mine paint it. Jacqueline Wilder."

"Jacqueline?"

"I don't think you know her. Jac and I have been friends for years."

"Jack?"

"She insisted on bringing the painting up herself so that I could surprise you. She left it with the folks in the camp office this afternoon. Oh, sweetheart, I hoped maybe—I don't know—that it would help bring us back together. A reminder of better times. You do like it, don't you?"

For a moment, he couldn't speak. Then a smile spread slowly across his face. "It's the nicest thing anyone has ever given me."

They made love a long time that night. Somewhere in the middle of all that passion, Cooper heard the sound of urgent voices coming from the direction of the sauna, but he paid no attention. Afterward, as Charlotte lay sleeping, he rose from their bed and went to the main room of the cabin. He took his notebook and a pen from among the writing materials he'd brought. He sat down at the table in the circle of light cast by the small lamp, and he began to write.

The words had not come so easily in years.

Jess Lourey

Jess Lourey is the author of the Murder-by-Month Mysteries, a humorous, small-town series featuring amateur sleuth Mira James. Knee High by the Fourth of July *is the most recent installment in the comical series. Lourey lives in Minnesota, where she teaches Creative Writing and Sociology full time at a two-year college. When not raising her wonderful kids, teaching, or writing, you can find her gardening and navigating the niceties and meanities of small-town life. She is a member of Mystery Writers of America, Sisters in Crime, The Loft, and Lake Superior Writers.*

The Locked Fish-cleaning House Mystery

Jess Lourey

Mrs. Berns pulled the last roller out of her apricot-tinged hair and watched with satisfaction as the poodle curl snapped to her skull. She traced perfect red arcs an inch above where her eyebrows used to be, spritzed rose water on her bony wrists, and adjusted the ties of her sparkly-white tennis shoes. Trip the light fantastic? She was going to take it down in a half nelson.

But first. She grabbed the Vaseline and slid a healthy dollop under the electronic band hanging loosely at the point just below her thumb where her wrist turned into her hand. With a practiced twist, Mrs. Berns was free. She tucked the band into the bed it was attached to, the bed she was expected to stay within ten feet of unless supervised by a nurse. Why this culture locked up its old people escaped her. So what if her kids had decided her late night roaming was a hazard? Apparently, she had done a shitty job raising that pack. Now it was up to her ingenuity to see her free of the nursing home, quietly, and into the waiting arms of Battle Lake.

Outside the antiseptic cage of the Senior Sunset, the late summer night was energizing. The water of the lake skirting the tiny town soaked the air with humidity and the smell of beach. It blended with the odor of wood smoke—someone burning leaves early?—and the spicy scent of the zinnias and marigolds bordering the sidewalk. Mrs. Berns studied her reflection in the side mirror of a Dodge Neon parked on the street. She looked good. The dance awaited.

A wedding dance in a resort was an exciting prospect. In theory, guests would only have to stumble to their cabins at the end of the festivities and so would have no hesitation about drinking their weight in cheap champagne and 3.2 beer. Mrs. Berns liked people-watching, but she loved drunk-watching. Given that the resort was located in town, on the west shore of the lake and within walking distance of the Senior Sunset, it would have been a crime for her to stay at the Sunset tonight.

Within a block of the resort, she heard the music calling to her, the siren song of Midwest wedding receptions: the Macarena. *When I dance, they call me macarena, and the boys, they say that I'm buena.* If she had had anything that jiggled besides skin, Mrs. Berns would be jiggling it. She settled for shaking her orange hair as she made her way down the hill, past the fish-cleaning house on her left and a smattering of cabins on the right. The resort lodge was packed top to bottom with Stevensons, the groom's family, locals every one of them. They were known in this area for two things: heavy drinking and heavier fishing. Instead of keeping up with the Joneses, people around here tried to keep up with the Stevensons.

Mrs. Berns headed to the open bar for a margarita and to get a view of the attendees. She didn't recognize a third of the people. Probably the bride's family. Must be one of them on the dance floor right now, taking great pride in the way her wide and slightly flat rear waved in the air—suggestive, but not lascivious, controlled with an edge—at just the right moment. Hand, hand on head; hand, hand around waist; hand, hand on rear; grind the air. Again and again, mechanically, her face tense with concentration. Mrs. Berns figured the dancer must have practiced the whole enchilada at home, angling two full-length mirrors just so.

Around here, the Macarena was a religion, and it was pounding to its crescendo. Laughing drunks shook to the beat on the dance floor and off, in sync for what was sure to be the only time tonight. The group was nearing its last ass slap, when *zziipp.* The music stopped abruptly, and the only sounds were mosquitoes buzzing

and ice melting. The crowd looked around, conf
their song gone? Who would dare interrupt thei
reached its climax?

The answer swayed next to the DJ booth, the
player cord in one of his hands and a microphe...
He had an announcement to make, and he didn't care who he
had to piss off to make it. In fact, it never occurred to him that
the crowd would rather dance than hear him talk. He grinned
lopsidedly, and the woman who had been dancing so feverishly
and joylessly just moments before glared at him, her thought as
clear as paint across her forehead. *Tell me that bastard didn't just stop
the Macarena.*

Mrs. Berns frowned at the dark-haired man with the mike.
Danny Stevenson, she thought to herself, *the drunk's drunk, the fishermen's fisherman, and the town manwhore.* His face still hung onto
what had passed for rugged good looks when he was young, and
in the right light, he looked like a smaller-nosed Harrison Ford.
At 5'11" he was not overweight, even though he had a baby Bud-
weiser gestating in his belly. The man was cute enough, and he
was persistent. Many women mistook that for love. His wife sure
had, fifteen years ago, when she agreed to join Dan in holy mat-
rimony. Poor Wendy.

"Hellloo." Dan gripped the microphone in one hand and
took up a sweating whiskey coke in the other. He over-enunci-
ated his words with the flair of a career drunk. "I'm Danny Boy,
and I just want to say that these-here newlyweds...where are they,
anyhow? Starting the honeymoon a little early?" He tried to make
an obscene gesture with his hands but, lacking the coordination,
settled for jacking the microphone up and down.

Most people went back to their drinks. The DJ took the opportunity to crouch behind his console and light a joint. He had been
saving it for the *Freebird-Stairway to Heaven* one-two punch he usually spun around midnight, but this interruption would distract the
crowd just as well.

Dan felt his audience slipping and cranked his show up a notch.
"Goddamn Battle Lake is beautiful. I'd like to thank the owners of

his-here resort for having us here to celebrate Mindy and Mike's union. Not many businesses brave enough to invite the whole Stevenson clan to a party! Whoop!"

Wendy rolled her eyes at her idiot husband and scratched her new tattoo, a bright yellow Long Shank Goldhead fly-fishing lure she'd had etched into her skin two weeks earlier. Wendy and Dan had achieved the impossible Minnesota dream a few years back—making a living as fishing guides—although they never worked the same resort. It had been at least a decade since they could stand the sight of each other, and if this hadn't been the wedding of her favorite cousin of Dan's, she would never have come. Wendy sucked deeply on her Eve Ultra Light Menthol and adjusted her bottle-black ponytail off her back and over her shoulder, where the crispy ends hung to her waist. Why couldn't the bastard do the world a favor and find some teenager to hit on in a dark corner, like he usually did?

As if he could read his wife's mind, Dan Stevenson dropped the microphone on the nearest table with an echoing clatter and chicken-danced up to a pair of tight-bodied and shiny young women. He had been trying to bait the interest of the Amazon, Brooke, all night, and now she was looking tipsy enough to bite. He tousled his hair so it looked just like that old actor everybody liked. When the DJ popped up and cued some Hall and Oates, he knew it was his night. *Damn, those boys could sing. Two white brothers with soul. What was the name of the song again?*

Troy saw the weaving Dan Stevenson stalk his girlfriend and snorted as he realized what song was playing. "Maneater." How totally fitting. Brooke had been chewing him up and spitting him out ever since they started dating two months ago. They had met at a street dance in Alexandria, and he had fallen for her, hook, line, and sinker. She was one of those girls who always looked clean and never went outside without a full face of make-up. He felt proud just standing next to her.

He had dated before. A lot, in fact, if you counted high school. The girls had always liked him because he was athletic. Troy was the best at baseball, so good he had almost played for the Alexandria Beetles, but his temper had gotten the best of him. One bad fight outside the Bugaboo Bay Nightclub two summers ago, and the farm team wouldn't touch him. He'd gotten a handle on it since then, he figured. When he felt the black rage build, he'd wiggle his toes and pretend he was out fishing or hunting, forcing his anger down the pole of a fishing rod or the barrel of a rifle until he caught and killed what he was after. In his mind, at least.

When Troy had met Brooke, it had been nearly two years since his last fight, and she felt like a good reward, with her red fingernails and fluffy hair. She was also tall, which, for a 6'5" guy, was a plus. And when she looked at him with that half smile, it almost started his pants on fire. It was enough to make him give up his dream of a 50" Plasma HDTV with a 3D Color Enrichment System and make a down payment on a promise ring.

Too bad she was a cheater. So far, she had made out with two of his friends and his stepbrother. She claimed it was the liquor that made her do it, and he was inclined to believe her. She really was a crazy drunk. When she was sober, she was the only woman for him, but jeez, how much could a guy take? He watched Brooke walk off with the lecher from the microphone and turned away. He was gonna have to do something, or his friends would say he was pussy-whipped, but he figured a couple shots of tequila first wouldn't kill anybody. He adjusted his balls, a bad habit he didn't know he had, and stalked off to the bar.

Across the room, Mrs. Berns shook her head happily. If she had read the situation right, Dan Stevenson was dancing up next to a whole world of hurt. Forget that the girl he was flirting with was six feet tall if she was an inch; it looked like her gorilla boyfriend, the one with the itchy package, was just about to get himself a tall glass of courage. Mrs. Berns rubbed her hands together. Tonight was really panning out. In her hurry to get another drink to better enjoy the show, she almost ran over a tiny blonde woman.

"Sorry, child! You should get some platform shoes, or they'll accidentally sweep you outta here with the trash." Mrs. Berns cackled and walked off.

"No prob," Celeste smirked to her back. Cut-rate pink Spumante dripped off her arm. "I'd much rather wear it than drink it." She slugged what was left in the glass and stared around the crowd. *Not a bad turnout,* she thought, but then again, she had no idea how many people had been invited. In fact, she didn't know anyone here. Coming to this wedding dance was what you'd call a side business for her. She could make four, maybe five hundred dollars picking pockets tonight.

Minnesota wedding dances were a gold mine. Celeste'd never seen so many farmers in a room, all of them with wallets full of cash because they didn't trust banks. She'd happened upon this knowledge just by chance, when her college roommate at Macalester had invited her to a cousin's wedding dance. The dance was in Paynesville, and it was her first small-town experience.

Up until then, she had gotten her thrills stripping at a Gentleman's Club in downtown Minneapolis. She hadn't had to do it, of course. Her dad was a successful defense attorney, and her mom, before she died, was a famous Twin Cities architect. The lack of necessity was what made it so exciting. Her therapist, the one her dad forced her to see after she was caught buying pot in north Minneapolis, diagnosed her with Adjustment Disorder. Celeste knew better. She just liked to have fun.

Once she found out how fun it was to steal from drunk farmers in Paynesville, she made a point of hitting as many small-town wedding dances as she could in the summer. They were easy to find. One just had to Google "Minnesota resorts," and a million websites would pop up, most of them listing when they were booked up for big parties. That's how she had found this resort, set on the northern edge of the town of Battle Lake.

Their website had encouraged her to "Bring the family and take home the memories." *No thanks,* she thought, when her eyes lighted on the "Welcome to the Stevenson Wedding Party, July 22nd!" *I'll just bring myself and take home the bacon.*

The hot night was perfect. People were drinking like sailors, trying to cool themselves off, and so numb from mosquito bites that they wouldn't notice a little tug on the back pocket of their dress pants. Celeste had been feeling good, alive and on fire, right up until old Danny Boy, the bloated dink from the microphone, had caught her hand as she was relieving him of his cash.

"Hey there, sweetcheeks. You didn't mean to steal from me, did you?"

His cow-brown eyes had glistened at her, traveling up and down her petite frame. She was used to men looking at her, but not for free. "Sorry. My mistake."

"Mistake?" He guffawed. "You were taking my wallet. I don't know where you're from, but around here, that's illegal." He dropped his voice to a whisper, and blew his whiskey-soaked breath into her ear. "I could be convinced to forget about it, though. Meet me by the fish-cleaning house in an hour."

"The fish-*cleaning* house?"

"Yeh, that little gazebo thing in the middle of the drive-around. In an hour." He winked and stumbled off.

That had been forty-five minutes ago, and Celeste figured it was about time to take him up on his offer. She knew how to deal with the sort of problem he presented.

She slid through the crowd just as the DJ decided it was time to crank the party up a notch. He programmed *Brick House* into his console and watched the melody work its magic. The big ladies got off their chairs, the kids started wiggling, and even the old men were working it. *The lady's stacked and that's a fact, ain't holding nothing back. She's a brick...house.*

"You got any of that left?"

The DJ raised an eyebrow at the orange-haired woman in front of him. She looked to be a couple years younger than God and was shaking her booty feverishly to the music as she spoke. "Any what?"

"Any of that wacky tabacky," Mrs. Berns crowed. She winked at him, and over his shoulder caught someone dropping a chicken wing off the buffet and sticking it back on the pile. "Don't worry, son. It's just between you and me."

The DJ had never smoked with an old lady before, but maybe she had glaucoma or something and he could help her out. He lit up, filling his booth with the sweet smell of burning grass, and was just about to hand it over when that teeny blonde chick he had been checking out earlier ran in screaming, "There's a dead body out there!" loud enough to drown out the funky music.

People poured out of the lodge like cattle. The DJ inserted

his long-playing 70s Disco Hits CD and followed Mrs. Berns. She wasn't afraid to use her elbows and soon found herself at the front of the crowd. The throng was making a perimeter around the closed fish-cleaning house, nobody daring to get within three feet of it to see what was inside, everyone unable to look away.

"It's not a blessed zoo display," Mrs. Berns said, stomping toward the tiny octagonal house. The smell hit her first, and it wasn't the sniff of a dead body. It was the stink of decades of fish scales and innards being scraped off and out in one tiny space. She walked through the wall of odor to the door and felt a whisper of a touch on her arm, as if she had broken through a spider web.

Mrs. Berns yanked on the door. It was latched from the inside. She stuck her head against the front screen, feet on tippy toes, and peered in. Sure enough, there was a big guy, face down, a knife in his back up to the hilt. Mrs. Berns saw blood and something white at the spot where the weapon had entered between his shoulder blades. She studied the crusty whiteness for a minute, in the flickering beam of the yard light, before she realized what it was. Frosting. Somebody had stabbed Danny Stevenson in the back with the wedding cake knife.

She walked around the fish-cleaning house and saw that the screens on all eight sides were nailed in at their edges. There was no hole in the wood making up the small building, and the seams with the roof were tight. It appeared as though Danny had gone into the cleaning house, locked the door, stabbed himself in the back, and fallen on his own dead face.

Mrs. Berns shook her head, hands on hips. She stared through the screen and across the interior of the house at the inside of the door, trying to imagine how it could have latched itself. The locking structure was simple—a 1" x 3" block of wood was nailed on one side and brought down into a wooden holder on the other side to keep one fisher from barging in on another—but you had to be inside to use it. That's when something bright caught her eye, a shiny object protruding from the block of wood barring entrance into the fish-cleaning house. It looked like one of the fishermen had stuck a three-pronged fishing lure into the wood, and it was the yard light reflecting off of it that had just caught Mrs. Berns's eye. It became immediately apparent to her who had killed Dan Stevenson, and how.

Mrs. Berns turned away from the hut. "You there, chickie," she said, indicating the tiny blonde whom she had earlier run into, and who had announced the dead body. The same tiny blonde who had been lifting wallets all night. "How'd you know he's dead?"

Celeste came forward. "Look at him. He's got a knife in his back."

"How'd you come across him?"

"He asked me to meet him at the fish-cleaning house. When I got here, the door was locked, and he was laying inside, just like he is now." Her eyes challenged the old lady to argue with her, but Mrs. Berns had no intention of doing so.

"And you two." Mrs. Berns pointed at Troy and Brooke, Itchy Nuts and the Amazon, who were huddled at the edge of the crowd, arm in arm. "You Sasquatches came together, but she hasn't been a good girl, have you, missy?"

Brooke shook her head, round heavy tears spilling onto her bronzed cheeks. "I followed that guy out here. His name was Danny, I think." Her voice cracked at the implications of using *was* in that sentence. "I just wanted to talk," she cut her eyes at Troy, "but Danny pulled me into that smelly hut and put his hands all over me. I slapped him and left."

Troy hugged her reassuringly. "I was at the bar when I heard the scream."

Mrs. Berns looked the two of them up and down. "You could be your own basketball team. That's okay. You're both off the hook," here she laughed at her own joke, "because it doesn't take an Einstein to see who killed Danny." Mrs. Berns nodded at the chain-smoking fisherwoman at the edge of the crowd, where she was filling her mouth with an Eve Ultra Light with one hand and scratching a bright yellow tattoo with the other. "Wendy, you come over here and hold something for me."

Wendy stared at Mrs. Berns sullenly, flipping her crunchy black hair to her back, where it covered her rear like a horse's tail. Her husband was dead, but her eyes were dry. "What?"

21

"Just come over here. I won't bite."

Wendy walked reluctantly out of the crowd, her eyes widening at the sound of a police siren. Someone had finally called the cops.

"Here it is," Mrs. Berns said, handing Wendy the nearly invisible fishing line strung through the hole of the screen opposite the door. It dangled about four feet off the ground, just high enough to whisper against Mrs. Berns's arm as she first walked to the cleaning house.

Wendy twitched when she saw the line but held on as directed. The crowd hushed as Mrs. Berns kicked around in the grass for a stick. When she found a thin branch, she fed it through the crack in the door and gently lifted the wooden block holding the entrance shut. When the block was fully upright, she slowly opened the door and warned Wendy not to let go of the line. As the door widened, the line in Wendy's hand was pulled forward, toward the door. The line was attached to the hook that was attached to the block of wood.

"Pretend that I'm your prize walleye, Wendy," Mrs. Berns said, letting the door slam shut. When it did, Wendy gave a yank on her line and pulled the block of wood back into place, effectively relocking the door.

"Whoever killed Danny stabbed him and then threaded a line through the screen and onto a fishing lure that they stuck into the wood, so it could be pulled shut behind them after they left. The Amazons are too tall—they would have strung the line out much higher—and blondie is too short, so that leaves you. That's your lure stuck in the wood, and your fishing line leading away from it, isn't it Wendy? And I bet if I looked in your pockets, I'd find the clippers you were going to use to cut the end so there'd be nothing hanging out for the police to find, but blondie must have come up on you too quick."

Wendy started shaking like a wet dog. "I always carry clippers in my pocket."

"You can tell it to the police, Wendy. None of us liked Danny Boy, but you would have been better off pushing him outta a boat. They don't call 'em fishing widows for nothing!" Mrs. Berns cackled and punched her way back through the crowd just as the Battle Lake Police car pulled up. She didn't want to be caught and dragged back to the Senior Sunset. The Minnesota night air she strode through smelled sweet and smoky, and she thought it was the perfect setting for a tango. She patted her apricot-colored hair into place, grabbed the DJ by the wrist, and led him back to the console with a smile on her lips and a wiggle in her hips. It was good to be alive.

Ellen Hart

Ellen is a five-time winner of the Lambda Literary Award for Best Lesbian Mystery, as well as a three-time winner of the Minnesota Book Award for Best Popular Fiction. Entertainment Weekly *recently named her one of the "101 movers and shakers in the gay entertainment industry." For the last eleven years, Ellen has taught "An Introduction to Writing the Modern Mystery" through the Loft Literary Center, the largest independent writing community in the nation. Her newest novels are* No Reservations Required, *A Sophie Greenway Mystery (June 2005) and* Night Vision, *A Jane Lawless Mystery (December 2006). She lives in Minneapolis with her partner of 29 years.*

14-A

Ellen Hart

I'm embarrassed to admit it, but I was always one of those women who believed that love, once found, would act like a kind of armor against all the ills of the world. I'd discovered my one true love in Curt, but over a period of years, I came to see that this romantic belief was nothing but illusion.

Love doesn't protect us. It opens us up, makes us a captive to the agony of small moments, gives us a way to interpret those moments but no means to protect ourselves from the pain of that knowing. And so, I want to tell you my story. As you no doubt already suspect, it's a cautionary tale. The death of love always is.

It all started seven years ago—on the first anniversary of our marriage.

September, 2000, Stone Point Resort

"Slow down," I said, looking over at Curt and seeing the intense concentration on his rugged face as he took the curve at sixty miles an hour—way too fast. We were on Highway 61, high above the North Shore of Lake Superior. It was a brilliant autumn day, made somewhat less lovely by my fear of imminent death.

"Baby, fast German cars are one of the last joys left to modern man. That—" He glanced at me. "—and beautiful women." He reached for my hand. "Happy anniversary, Laurie."

Curt and I had been married one year ago today—his second marriage, my first. At thirty-one, I was eleven years his junior, but the age difference wasn't an issue. His energy was so infectious—

and so constant—that it was already wearing me out. Pretty soon, I figured, our physical ages would be about the same. When I turned sixty, he would likely be only in his fifties. Something to do with physics—inertia, or lack thereof. But life with Curt was worth every minute of my accelerating wear and tear. I never thought I'd have this kind of passion in my life and I intended to hang on to it—even if it meant closing my eyes and white-knuckling it as we sped around sheer rock cliffs.

"If I knew where we were going it would help," I said.

Curt raised a blond eyebrow. "I have ziss little cabin in za voods, my dear. Very remote. No one vill hear za screams."

"You are so full of it."

"True. But I do have a surprise."

I thought I knew what that surprise was. I'd always enjoyed spending time on the shore so I figured we'd turn off the road at some little resort, spend a few days relaxing in a semi-grungy cabin, drinking a lot of wine and making love.

Since moving to Duluth seven months ago, we hadn't had a chance to take a real vacation. Curt had been the vice president of a financial firm in Minneapolis when I first met him, already well established and successful in his career. I assumed we would settle in the Twin Cities, but when the company opened a Duluth office, Curt jumped at the chance to manage it. My work is portable so we moved into a beautiful home up near UMD in east Duluth a few months later and I set up my studio in a well-lit room above the garage. I'm a sculptor. Welded metal. Not a very feminine pursuit, but one that suits me just fine. I'm making a name for myself, too. It's slow, but it's happening.

A couple miles past Lutsen, Curt slowed the car. He eventually pulled off next to a sign that said STONE POINT RESORT, NO VACANCY. We bumped down a dirt road that brought us to a narrow paved parking area. A line of new townhouses, just a few hundred yards from a rocky beach, loomed directly in front of us.

"Hope you made a reservation," I said.

"Oh, golly gee. I never thought of that."

I socked him on the arm.

After he cut the motor, we sat for a moment and looked

around. The long row of townhouses was stained a deep redwood color. The trim was pale yellow. It struck me as sort of "Victorianna meets North Woods." The individual roofs were all steeply pitched, covered with golden wood shingles. Double doors sat back from the individual steps under smaller vaulted overhangs. At the end of the row was a truck loaded with firewood. Looking a little closer, I saw that each unit had its own protected cubby under the steps, where the firewood was kept. A workman stood outside of the truck, feeding wood into the cubbies.

The workman waved as we got out.

Curt waved back, and then pressed his hand behind me and guided me up to the door.

"Shouldn't we get the luggage?"

"I'll take care of that in a minute." He produced a key from the pocket of his leather jacket and opened the door. The sign above it said, 14-A

"These were built just last year," he said, flipping on a light as we walked down a hallway, passing the bedroom and the bathroom on our way to the main living area. Floor-to-ceiling windows overlooked the lake and just about took my breath away.

"This is unbelievable," I said, turning around, taking it all in.

The sunken living room and dining room were flanked by a rock fireplace, a large screen TV, and a wall unit filled with electronics. A small deck, again sunken so that it didn't spoil the view, jutted off the front. I'd never seen anything like this on the shore before. Most of the resorts were pretty rustic.

"You like it?" Curt asked.

"Are you kidding me? This is my idea of roughing it." I'd grown up poor, so Stone Point Resort felt like a penthouse at the Hilton.

"There's a Jacuzzi in the bathroom. And they've got two good-sized pools—one outdoors, and one inside. And a wonderful restaurant down at the main lodge—and an upstairs bar, all with incredible views of the lake. Oh, and just up on the road, there's this special little cafe that serves great homemade breakfasts. And a bottle shop. And—"

"I'm never leaving," I said.

"Well, actually, we don't have to." He dropped the keys into my hand. "We're the proud new owners."

"Huh?" I turned to stare at him. "I thought these were rental units."

"They are, but you can buy them too. Stone Point Resort rents them out. It's all part of the deal."

I'm sure my lower jaw must have hit the floor.

Curt grinned, pulled me into his arms, twirled me around. "I wanted to surprise you. I've spent a lot of time doing the research. This is our first big investment as a married couple, Laurie. Renting the place to vacationers helps defray the mortgage, which is pretty hefty, I will admit, but we can handle it. It's a win–win deal, babe. And we get to use it whenever we want. 'Course, we have to make reservations in advance, block out weeks or weekends when we'll want to drive up here. But if we feel like coming up, we can always call and see if anyone's booked the place. If not, it's all ours."

"You don't have to sell me on it."

"Wanna see the bedroom?"

Right around then, I forgot about the luggage.

Four Years Later: October, 2004, Stone Point Resort

Curt was outside on the balcony grilling hamburgers for our lunch. I was inside, drinking a cup of coffee and gazing out the front windows at the gloomy fall afternoon. As a child, I'd always hated the fall because it meant an end to my summer vacation. Now I hated it for other reasons. Autumn was a time of endings. Everything around me felt as if it was struggling to produce one last burst of color before the cold winds of November arrived to blow it all away.

I guess my life felt a little like that too. For the past year I'd been working like crazy, producing some of the best work I'd ever done. I was counting on being invited to do a show at the famous Mason-Brett Gallery in New York—my first chance at the big leagues. The owner of the gallery had flown to Minnesota to look at my work. She'd been so positive, so flattering, that I'd come to think of it as a sure thing. And then last week my agent had called and said it was a no-go. The rejection sent me into a tailspin. I'd been counting on it for so long that I felt like my career had hit a wall. It seemed the only part of my life that was rock solid was my marriage. Curt and I had never been happier. Well, with one exception.

It was a heartbreak for both of us. For the past five years, we'd been trying to conceive a child. At first, we both thought it was just a matter of time. But during the third year, we'd been tested and Curt learned that he had a low sperm count. A child wasn't impossible, but it would be difficult. The stress this produced on our marriage had taken a toll. My biological clock was just about to strike midnight, and so this getaway to the shore was supposed to be a time to reevaluate our priorities.

"Break out the beer," said Curt, coming through the door with a small tray of burgers.

We stood in the kitchen and fixed ourselves plates of food, then sat down in the living room by the big windows. Curt had built a fire. He was trying his best to cheer me up about the gallery thing, and I loved him for it.

After taking a long pull on his beer, Curt said, "You know, Laurie, if we don't ever have a child, it's not the end of the world."

"Then why does it feel like it?"

He chewed for a few seconds, trying to come up with an answer. "Do you blame me?"

"Oh, honey. No. Don't ever feel that way."

"But you want a child and I can't give you one. Makes me feel like a failure."

"You're the best man I've ever known. You could never be a failure. It's nobody's fault, Curt. It's just the way it is." I looked at the food on my plate. I wasn't the least bit hungry.

"You've had a bad week. Maybe we should forget about reassessing stuff and just have some fun." He tried a smile.

I forced one in return. He was so handsome, a lock of sandy blond hair falling across his forehead. My mother would tell me I needed to count my blessings. And my mother, as usual, would be right.

After lunch, Curt loaded the fireplace with a couple more logs, then laid down on the couch to read one of his financial magazines. I worked in the kitchen for a few minutes, cleaning up the dishes, putting away the uneaten food. When I was done, I sat down by the fire and picked up the journal we left in the unit for guests.

Stone Point Resort encouraged guest journals. Most of the units had them. We were on our third—the first two having been filled with vacationer's thoughts on their hiking experiences, the good and bad restaurants they'd found, and the joy they received from staying at such a beautiful resort. Some people even thanked us. I never really understood that. I mean, it wasn't as if we were opening our home to them, or that they weren't paying premium prices to stay here, and yet some people felt exactly that way. They commented on the furnishings, the artwork—which had all been a done deal before I ever walked into the place. The resort had rules about what dishes could be used, what glassware, chairs, pictures on the wall—everything. I liked the knotty pine walls and the North Woods feel, but it hadn't been any of my doing.

Opening the book to the last few entries, I smiled when I saw a child's scrawl, and a couple of drawings, one of a bear and the other a gull. "I'm 8. I live in Minneapolis. I like the lake. Signed, Amy." Curt seemed so engrossed in what he was reading that I decided not to interrupt him. I moved on to the next comment.

"Curt?" I said after a few seconds.

"Hmm?"

"I think you should see this."

"See what?"

"What someone wrote in the journal."

He put the magazine down. "Is it funny?"

I shook my head.

"Read it to me."

I turned toward him. "Rich people are pigs. You think you own the world, that you can do anything you damn well please and someone else will clean up the mess. You've probably never done a hard day's work in your life. I don't know how someone gets the kind of money to buy a place like this, but it's not right. Every time you come, you look right through me, like I'm nobody. I'm invisible. But maybe that's a good thing, because I see what you do. I'm a witness. You're everything a truly moral person would hate. Just remember, there's a judgment day waiting."

"Jesus," said Curt. "What a nut case."

"It's more than that," I said.

"It must be one of the staff. Maybe it's that red-haired housekeeper who always glares at us when we ask for more towels, or one of the groundskeepers." He sat up, tossed the magazine on the coffee table. "People are weird."

He didn't seem to get it. "Honey, that was a threat."

"You mean the part about judgment day? The person's obviously some religious wacko. Thinks we'll fry in lower hell one day."

"But judgment day could mean something else, something this guy plans to do. To us."

"Could have been a man or a woman," he mused. "Whatever the case, I don't think it's anything to worry about."

"Look, Curt, I'll never feel comfortable staying here again, not until we find out who made the threat."

"I think you're blowing this way out of proportion."

I stared at him until he got the point.

"Okay, okay. If it will make you feel better, I'll run it over to the office, see what Jim Benson thinks." Jim was one of the four men who owned the resort.

"I'll go with you. I'm not staying here alone."

A few minutes later, we were sitting in front of Jim's desk, watching him read the message.

"Let me keep the book," he said. "I'll see if I can match the handwriting to someone on our staff. But, honestly, I don't think it's anything to worry about."

"Are you saying it's happened before?" I asked. "Other units have received notes like this?"

He scratched his balding head. "Well, nothing exactly like this. But, yeah, occasionally we'll see something nasty—or just plain strange. I always say just remove the journal and start a new one. We've never had any serious problems. Whoever wrote that crap in your book was probably just havin' a bad day."

I couldn't understand why everyone was minimizing my concerns. "It scares me," I said.

"I'll do everything in my power to get to the bottom of it," Jim said. "In the meantime, have dinner on us tonight at The Cove."

"And a bottle of champagne?" Curt said, eyebrows raised.

"Hell, why not."

Three Years Later: August, 2007, Minneapolis

I drove down to the Twin Cities from Duluth during the third week in August to spend some time with my mom. Curt was out of town on a business trip, and I didn't like staying by myself in that big, drafty old house. I often came down when he was gone. But this time, I had a real reason for the visit. Mom had fallen and broken a bone in her foot. She lived alone, and was feeling miserable and sorry for herself. Her foot was in a cast, so she was able to get around, but the pain pills made her sleepy, and the cast made it impossible for her to drive. My sister in Ohio was driving up the next week to stay with her. I think all the attention made Mom feel special, and that was fine with me.

The first night I got grilled on how everything was going in my life. My marriage. My art. I still hadn't been able to break into the New York art scene, but my agent had informed me we were getting some nibbles from a gallery in London. I told my mother that I might bypass New York altogether and go straight to Europe. She warned me against being too headstrong, too impatient. She had that one right. I was both. And I also sensed in myself something darker—a growing anger. Not only was I furious that the art world seemed to be passing me by without even giving me a chance to show what I could do, but being unable to conceive a child felt like a huge, secret fissure in the foundation of my life. Over the past few years, it seemed like something in the structure of things had subtly turned against me. By now, Curt and I had given up on having a child. But the loss—and I felt it as a loss—was like an acid eating away at me.

"Cut yourself some slack, Laurie," my mom said over the dinner table that night. "Remember, count your blessings."

"Right."

"You've got a wonderful husband."

My smile was cheerless, even resentful.

"Stop all this feeling sorry for yourself, honey." She poked my arm, grinned. "That way lies madness."

I laughed. It was an old joke. One of her favorite sayings. My mom had a lot of favorite sayings. I used to like them, even believed them, but now they seemed pretty threadbare.

The fact was, telling her about Curt and me was even more of a problem. In the last year, we'd begun to grow apart. Curt said I was making my usual mountain out of a molehill. That marriages went through phases. We couldn't be newlyweds forever. Maybe he was right. I truly didn't know anymore. I just knew I wanted what we once had back.

The next day I went to the grocery store to pick up some things for Mom. While I was standing at the meat counter, looking at the chuck roasts, I spied a familiar face talking to one of the butchers. It was Andrea, Curt's first wife. I'd met her once, before Curt and I were married, and had seen lots of pictures of her. I knew she lived in south Minneapolis, but never thought I'd run into her.

When she was done talking, she turned my way. Her face sobered as our eyes locked. Neither one of us could politely back away, so I smiled.

"Andrea. Hi."

She walked over. Andrea was a short woman, not quite fat, but moving steadily in that direction. She didn't seem like the kind of woman Curt would ever be interested in, but when they were first married, she was younger. Youth was better than any make-up ever invented.

"Laurie," she said, not even trying to hide her snide tone. "How are you?"

"Great. Really great."

Just then, a boy rushed up to her. "Mom, can I get that new cereal I told you about? It's got vitamins in it, so it's good for you."

I stared at him. "You have a son?" He looked about eight. Healthy. Dark-haired. Beautiful.

"Jeremy, this is Laurie. A...person...I—"

"Hey," he said, not quite smiling, impatient for an answer. "The cereal?"

"I suppose," she said, without taking her eyes off me.

"I didn't know you had a son."

"He's not Curt's. I remarried."

"I know. You're lucky to have him. I've always wanted children."

She snorted. "Well, then you sure married the wrong guy."

"What's that mean?"

"Curt never wanted children—it would spoil his lifestyle, cut down on his play time. When you're a kid yourself, you don't want to share your toys."

"Curt wanted a child as much as I did. It just didn't happen."

"Oh, pu-leeze. If he'd wanted a child, he wouldn't have had a vasectomy when he was twenty-three."

"He what?" I was so shocked that for a moment, I almost couldn't speak. "That's impossible. He has a low sperm count. That's why—"

"I don't know what kind of line he's been feeding you, but we slept together for six years without contraception. He doesn't have a low sperm count, he has a nonexistent sperm count."

My mouth opened but nothing came out.

"You're just the kind of woman he was looking for. Stupid and gullible. I thought forty-one was kind of young to marry a trophy wife, but you sure fit the bill."

"Are you crazy? I'm not a trophy wife."

"Lady, wake up and smell the coffee. I'm not even sure you know who you married. Women like you are pathetic. Plastic to the core."

I grabbed hold of her arm and squeezed hard. "Take that back."

She shoved me away. "You lay another finger on me and I'll sue you and that bastard husband of yours for everything you've got."

I wanted to smash her face in. "You're lying. You want to hurt me, but it won't work. Take your son and waddle off into the sunset, you freaking blimp. Oh, and don't forget your six bags of potato chips. Wouldn't want to starve yourself in front of the TV tonight."

She just smiled. "Ask Curt about the vasectomy."

September, 2007, Stone Point Resort

Before I found the threatening message in the journal, I used to come up to the shore by myself occasionally, especially when Curt was out of town on a business trip. But after Jim Benson tried to find the author of the note and failed, I told Curt I'd only come up with him. I'm not a weak woman, but that note truly frightened me.

This weekend was to be our late summer getaway. We lugged our suitcases into the bedroom and got everything arranged. As Curt was building a fire in the living room fireplace, the nasty redheaded housekeeper knocked on the door to tell us there was a leak in the bathroom shower and that the new handyman would come by later to fix it.

"New handyman?" I said, a question in my voice.

"The guy who delivers wood. He was just hired full-time. He's been subbing for years when our main guy gets too busy. He's nice and quiet, so he won't bother you."

As if she cared. I was about to thank her when she turned abruptly and walked away. Maybe she was in a perpetual bad mood, or maybe she just didn't have any social skills. Curt called from the living room with the suggestion that I make us a drink. It sounded good to me. Because we're the owners, we have a couple locked closets and a cabinet in the kitchen to store things we use whenever we come up. I unlocked the cabinet door and was about to pull out the whiskey and sweet vermouth when I noticed a folded piece of paper that had slipped down between the gin and the vodka bottles. I pulled it out and flipped it open.

"Where's my drink?" asked Curt, sounding thirsty.

I turned to look at him, then returned my attention to the note. Pressing it into the pocket of my sweater, I got down two glasses.

"What were you reading?" he asked, stepping up into the kitchen.

"Nothing," I said. But he could tell from the look on my face that it was hardly "nothing."

"What was it?"

"You wouldn't be interested."

"Let me see it." He adjusted his glasses and read it out loud. "Judgment day is at hand. I warned you and now you're going to 'reap the wild wind.'"

"Fuck this," said Curt. For once, he actually looked upset.

"Aren't you going to tell me it's nothing?" Over the last few months, I'd begun to wonder if Curt had been behind that threat in the journal. He knew it would upset me. Maybe he didn't want me coming up to Stone Point without him—or more specifically, unannounced.

I wasn't as naive when it came to my husband as I once was.

"I'm taking this over to Benson. This time, we're either getting some action or I'll sue."

"I'm not staying here," I said.

"Put on your coat and come with me."

"No, I mean I'm not staying here tonight. This weekend. Not with some weirdo out there watching us, waiting for a chance to...to—"

Curt drew me into his arms. "I'll figure this out, honey, I promise."

"I want to go home."

"Okay. I understand. Let's take everything back out to the car. But before we go, we'll stop at the main lodge and I'll show this to Jim. Demand he talk to the police."

"Doesn't matter. I'm never coming back here."

"Can't you just give it a little time, let me see what I can do? Why do you have to be so 'all or nothing?'"

"It's the way I am, Curt. I guess you can take it or leave it." Not exactly loving words. But by then, the love I'd once felt for him was gone.

November, 2007, Duluth

Curt was on one of his business trips when I got the call. It was just after nine in the evening.

"Mrs. Richardson?"

"Yes?"

"This is Officer Yager with the Cook County police. I'm afraid

I have some bad news. It's been sleeting up here on and off all day. Your husband and a friend were driving on Highway 61 when their car apparently skidded off the road. I'm sorry, ma'am." There was a long pause. "They're both gone."

I switched the phone to my other ear and sat down. "No, it must be someone else. My husband's in Milwaukee on business."

"Your husband's name is Curt? Curt Richardson? Drives a red Audi two-door roadster?"

"Yes, but it can't be him."

"I'm sorry, ma'am. His body has been taken to Cook County North Shore Hospital in Grand Marais."

"I…I don't—" I took a breath. "And the person with him?"

"A woman. According to her driver's license, her name was Sylvia Conrad, from Duluth. Did you know her?"

"No," I said. "I have no idea who she is."

"We found a plastic key card in your husband's pocket. It was for Stone Point Resort."

"We own a unit up there. 14-A."

"That explains it." He hesitated. "Look, Mrs. Richardson, I don't want to upset you any more than I already have, but I've seen a lot of cars go off the road in bad weather. There were some skid marks on the road this time that looked…well, suspicious. This may seem like it's coming out of nowhere, but did your husband have any enemies?"

"No, of course not."

"Nobody ever threatened him?"

"No. Well, except—"

The police officer waited.

"You should talk to the owner of Stone Point Resort—Jim Benson. My husband and I received some odd, handwritten notes in our condo. Mr. Benson has them."

"Can you be more specific?"

"We received two. One back in 2004. It was sort of garbled. Someone thought we were pigs, that we were rich and arrogant. The note talked about a judgment day. And then we found another one a couple months ago from the same person. They'd slipped it through a crack in one of the locked cabinets we use for liquor.

Same thing. Only this time, it said that judgment day was at hand. I told my husband I refused to go up there anymore. I was too scared."

"Thanks for the tip. If you're planning to drive up—"

"Of course I am. I have to!"

"I'd wait until tomorrow. The roads should be better by then."

"No, I'm coming tonight. I have to see him."

"It's not pretty, Mrs. Richardson. Maybe you should bring a friend along. Oh, the car was towed to a lot in Tofte."

"I don't care about the car."

"No, of course not." He gave me a number where he could be reached and then hung up.

A couple hours later I pulled my BMW into the parking lot outside our townhouse. I used my key card to let myself in. The interior was dark, so I switched on the hall light. As I walked into the bedroom I could smell the woman's perfume. Maybe it was wishful thinking, but it smelled cheap. Clothes were strewn all over the floor. A sexy nightgown hung in the closet next to one of Curt's business suits. I touched the suit and felt the hard shell I'd been living in for months begin to crack.

And that's when I heard it. Floorboards creaking. The sound of heavy footsteps walking down the hall. I moved back into the shadows, my heart pounding so hard in my ears I thought the sound would give me away.

A tall, strongly-built man moved into the doorway. It was the man who delivered the wood. The new handyman. "I know you're here," he said. His voice was deep. Rough. "I saw your car outside."

I couldn't exactly hide. I had no weapon, no way to protect myself if he wanted to hurt me. "What do you want?" I asked. My voice shook.

He pulled off his baseball cap, held it in his hands. "Your husband was a bastard. I wanted to tell you so many times that he was bringing women up here on the side. I tried to scare him with those notes I wrote. Your husband—I mean, did you know?"

"Not until a few months ago."

"He was slick, all right. Never brought the same woman twice.

If there's anything else I can do—"

"Anything else?" I couldn't see him very well, so I inched a step closer.

"Sure," he said. "I'm the handyman. I fix things."

I wasn't positive, but in the dim light I thought I saw him smile.

We stood staring at each other for a few more seconds, and then I sat down on the bed. When I finally realized what was in my heart, it almost took my breath away.

Looking up at him, I hesitated a moment, and then said, "Thank you."

David Housewright

A reformed newspaper reporter and ad man, Housewright earned the 1996 Edgar Award for Best First Novel from the Mystery Writers of America as well as a Shamus nomination from the Private Eye Writers of America for Penance. *His second novel,* Practice To Deceive, *won the 1998 Minnesota Book Award. He followed those efforts with* Dearly Departed, A Hard Ticket Home, Tin City *(2006 Minnesota Book Award nominee),* Pretty Girl Gone, *and* Dead Boyfriends. *His short stories have appeared in publications as diverse as* Ellery Queen's Mystery Magazine *and* True Romance *as well as anthologies* The Silence of the Loons *and* Twin Cities Noir.

Miss Behavin'

David Housewright

The waitress said, "That's a pretty ring."

Kathryn held her hand up and examined the ring like she was seeing it for the first time. The diamond sparkled in the light.

"Thank you," she said.

"How long have you kids been married?"

The question startled her. She flashed a panicked gaze at her companion sitting across the table.

"Thirteen years," he said.

"Good for you." The waitress finished refilling their water glasses and left to serve other customers. Kathryn watched her drift across the restaurant. A strand of black hair fell against her cheek when her head swung back to the table and she smoothed it into place.

"She thought we were married," Kathryn said.

"We are married," her companion said.

"But not to each other."

"A minor technicality."

"Is that all it is?"

"Kathryn, it's all perfectly innocent. If anyone asks."

"Like your wife, Dr. Markham?"

"Yes, like my wife," Markham said. "If anyone asks, I'll tell them I met an interesting, intelligent woman during a seminar at a pharmaceutical convention and we had lunch together in plain sight of everyone. So, what do you think about the new beta-blockers, Doctor?"

"I'm surprised you even remember what the seminar was about considering the way you kept staring at my legs."

"They are magnificent."

Markham liked the way Kathryn's cheeks flamed at the compliment, liked the way she smiled coyly and looked away. Doctors were all the same, he believed. No matter how generous, considerate, or kindly they might seem, they were still doctors, which meant they were smarter than everyone else and sooner or later they would need to prove it. Kathryn was trying to prove it now, trying to prove how sophisticated and worldly she was. Like during the seminar when she noticed Markham noticing her. She leaned across two seats and whispered, "May I help you?"

"Just looking," Markham said.

"See anything you like?"

"One or two things, but I prefer to conduct a full examination before I make a final diagnosis."

"Perhaps a joint consultation is called for."

It was Kathryn who suggested lunch. The drug companies sponsoring the four-day convention insisted that the physicians and other guests attend all the morning seminars, yet afternoons and evenings were free for fun and frolic. Only Kathryn was over her head. To her surprise Markham had taken her flirting seriously and pressed hard. She would now either have to run for cover or make good on her innuendoes. Markham was betting on the latter. He had been convinced from the moment Kathryn walked into the meeting room and searched carefully before selecting his row, that she could be had.

"We're so lucky with the weather," Kathryn told him. "I expected northern Minnesota to be much colder. How far are we from Canada?"

"About forty miles as the crow flies."

"Where I come from, most people think Minnesota is somewhere up around the Arctic Circle. But it's really quite lovely."

"Lovely," Markham repeated. He was looking directly in her eyes when he said the word so she wouldn't be mistaken about what he meant. She smiled and glanced away again. Works every time, he told himself.

"Tell me about your wife," Kathryn said.

This time it was Markham's turn to look away. He wasn't embarrassed or surprised; sooner or later the question always came up. He was merely buying time while he selected the desired response: soft, hard, or harder? Some women preferred to hear nasty tales about the wife. They wanted to make sure they weren't breaking up a happy home. Markham thought it made being the other woman easier for them to bear. Hey, the bitch deserves it. Yet, Kathryn seemed different. The way she averted her eyes when he complimented her, the way she suddenly seemed fearful that they would be seen together, what the waitress would think. Kathryn was concerned with consequences. First do no harm. Soft, he decided.

"Susan is very smart, very beautiful, and I love her more than I have words to tell," Markham said.

"But."

"Hmm?"

"I heard a 'but' in that sentence."

"You're a doctor," Markham said. "You know how punishing the profession can be. The hours. The interrupted dinners. The ruined holidays. At first it seemed like Susan enjoyed being a doctor's wife, yet after a few years she decided she needed more. She wanted to have her own identity, her own career. I was all for it. I encouraged her to go back to school; encouraged her to get her master's. Only now it seems what she really wanted all along was to stop being a doctor's wife."

"Is that why you're flirting with a woman you barely know?"

"Well, it helps that the woman is lovely and smart." He was taking a helluva chance, Markham knew. Still, they were staying at a resort casino after all—slot machines, blackjack tables, poker rooms, even bingo. "Why are you flirting with a man you barely know?" he asked.

"Because…" She shook her head like it was a subject too painful to discuss. "Because the man is handsome and smart. Let it go at that."

"I didn't come here looking for a fling."

"But you could be talked into it."

"You could talk me into it."

"I haven't done—I've never tried to do anything like this before."

"Anything like what?"

"Seduce a man I don't know."

He shoots, he scores, Markham's inner voice shouted. "Well, it worked," he said aloud.

"Has it?"

"I know I'm having a very difficult time keeping my hands off you."

Kathryn glanced discreetly about the restaurant, trying to examine every face while pretending not to. Finally, she asked, "What are your plans for the rest of the day?"

"I was scheduled to play golf, but I'd rather spend time with you."

"No, play golf." Kathryn's voice was emphatic. "If you break your appointments, people will wonder why and I won't become a source of gossip. People know me here and I don't want them to think that we're, that we're..."

"Sleeping together?"

Kathryn pushed back her chair. The legs made a scraping sound on the carpet that caused Markham's heart to jump. She's getting away. "I'm sorry if I offended you," he said.

"I'm not offended," Kathryn said. "But people talk, don't they?"

"Kathryn..."

"I want to be with you, only not in a crowd. Not so anyone can see."

"I'm open to suggestions."

"Give me your cell phone number. I'll call and tell you where I am."

"When?"

"Whenever. You'll take the call and tell whomever you're with that something requires your immediate attention—that's what doctors do, right? They run off to things that require their immediate attention."

"What if I can't get away?"

"Then that will be the end of that."

Markham slid his business card across the table and the woman slipped it into her bag. "You don't strike me as a woman who plays games, Kathryn," he said.

"Consider it a test of character, Doctor. If you pass, who knows, tomorrow I might let you sit next to me at the seminar for Angiogenesis Inhibitors in Clinical Trials."

"Will we hold hands?"

Kathryn rose from her chair. Her voice was loud and clear. "It was a pleasure to meet you, Doctor."

Markham also stood. He extended his hand. "The pleasure was entirely mine, Doctor," he said.

"You pay for lunch," Kathryn whispered.

Markham watched as she glided out of the restaurant and disappeared into the resort. "That went well," he said to no one in particular.

Markham signaled for the check. Before it arrived, a tall, thin man dressed like he was going sailing slid into the chair that Kathryn had occupied.

"Who was that?"

"Gee, Stephen. Don't be shy. Have a seat."

"Thank you, I will."

"French fry?"

Markham pushed Kathryn's plate forward. She had eaten the entire teriyaki chicken sandwich she had ordered, yet didn't touch the rest of the meal.

Stephen took three fries and stuffed them into his mouth. He spoke around them. "So, who was that?"

"A doctor from Arizona." Markham couldn't remember where in Arizona; he hadn't been listening that hard when Kathryn told him. "We met at the seminar this morning."

"Why were you having lunch with her?"

Markham stared at the man over the rim of his iced tea. "Just comparing notes," he said.

"Of course," Stephen said. "Silly question. Her legs didn't factor into it at all."

"Stephen…"

"Are you going to tell Susan about her?"

"I don't tell Susan about everyone I have lunch with. How about you?"

That last was less a question than it was an accusation and Stephen knew it. He smiled and ate a few more fries. "I only tell her about the women," he said.

"What's your story, anyway?" Markham asked.

"When Susan learned that we were both attending the same medical convention, she told me to keep an eye on you." As he spoke, he pointed two fingers at his eyes, turned them and pointed the same fingers at Markham's eyes, then repeated the gesture twice more.

"Stop it," Markham said.

"Just looking out for my sister-in-law's interests."

"The fact that your brother is married to Susan's sister does not make you her brother-in-law."

"Honorary brother-in-law."

Markham sighed deeply, dramatically. Stephen snooping around with Kathryn about to call at any minute. I need this, he told himself. I really do.

"You have no right to interpose yourself into my affairs," he said.

"Affairs. What a splendid way to put it."

"Stephen, I don't know how you got it into your head that I'm cheating on Suz…"

"You've done it before."

The check came. Markham scribbled his room number and name across it and gave it back to the waitress. He waited for her to depart before he spoke.

"That's past history. Susan and I have dealt with the issue and moved on. Not that it's any of your business, but you should do the same."

"You've cheated before. You'll do it again."

"Seriously, Stephen. This jealousy of yours, it's getting old. Susan's married to me. She loves me. I know you have this fantasy of the two of you running away together, but it's not going to happen."

"If you were out of the picture—"

"Not going to happen. If Susan wanted a divorce all she'd have to do is ask. Only she doesn't want a divorce. She didn't want one when things between us were rocky. She won't ask for one now when our marriage is solid."

"Good Catholic girls like Susan don't get divorced."

"Then you're screwed, aren't you, pal?" Markham rose from the table and gave the other man a playful slap on the back. "We need to find you a girl."

★ ★ ★

Markham shot a half dozen strokes above his handicap, costing him $65 and bragging rights to the two doctors and a pharmaceutical rep that completed his foursome. He blamed Kathryn. Every time he tried to visualize his shot, he would see her—usually in various stages of undress. Plus, there were the dozen times he checked his cell phone. Only he didn't use her as an excuse, instead asking the other golfers, "Did I tell you about my sore shoulder?" every time he shanked a ball. Discretion—he figured that was the least he could give her considering what she was about to give him. Besides, he told himself, with Stephen on the prowl he needed to be careful.

After seeing to his clubs, Markham joined his companions on the outdoor patio adjacent to the clubhouse. Three rounds of drinks were consumed, all paid for with the money he had lost. While he joked and drank he thought he saw someone he knew on the short staircase that led from the patio to the rich, green golf course. But the woman's back was turned and she quickly descended the steps before he could get a good look at her. Still, his stomach had an express-elevator-going-down feeling and his face became pale enough that the pharmaceutical rep asked, "Are you feeling all right?"

"Fine," Markham said. "I was just remembering the double-bogey on 13." His friends all thought that was pretty funny and a moment later he was laughing, too.

The resort was divided into five parts, the golf course and clubhouse, Heritage Center, marina, casino, and resort. From where he sat, Markham could see the roof and upper floors of the latter two buildings. After the third round, the golfers went their separate ways. Markham drifted toward the resort, about a short par four away. As he rounded the clubhouse he heard a voice. "Hello, Doctor." Markham pivoted toward it. Barely ten feet stretched between him and the woman he was sure he had seen on the staircase. Only he was nothing if not adaptable. Instead of showing fear, this time Markham forced a smile.

"Caroline," he said. He moved forward and engulfed her in his arms. She didn't resist the hug, but she didn't hug him back, either. "What are you doing here?"

"My job," Caroline said.

There was rancor in her voice. Markham pretended not to hear it. Seeing her in Northern Minnesota was unexpected, certainly. Still, he was a doctor. He was trained to deal with the unexpected.

"That's right," Markham said. He kissed her cheek. "You work for the drug company."

"You remember."

"Of course, I remember. I only wish I had known you were here earlier. We could have had lunch. We could have had breakfast." He gave that last word added emphasis. They had had breakfast together once before.

Caroline folded her arms across her chest. "You never called," she said.

"I wanted to. I must have picked up the phone a dozen times."

"But you didn't call."

"How could I, sweetie?" Markham's voice was suddenly filled with regret. "Were we together? Were we ever going to be together? You knew about Susan. You knew…"

Markham turned his head away so the young woman couldn't see the tears that would have been in his eyes if only he had learned how to cry on cue. Something to work on, he told himself. Maybe take an acting class. He felt Caroline's hand on his arm. He covered it with his own hand and gave it a squeeze.

"Is she any better?" Caroline's voice had changed, too. It swung from animosity to commiseration, just as Markham had predicted. Caroline, he knew, could be had.

"No. She had been taking these drugs…"

"Tysabri?" Caroline asked.

"And the Interferons. They don't seem to do much good. She just gets weaker and weaker. She's so tired all the time. She hates it."

"My mother had MS, too."

"You have every right to be angry, Caroline."

"No, no…"

"Only what could I do? Desert my chronically ill wife because I found love with a younger, more beautiful woman? How could I do that to Susan? What kind of man would I be? You wouldn't want to be with a man like that."

"No, you can't leave her."

"And calling you, hearing your voice, knowing we couldn't be together. It was just too much to bear."

Markham hugged the woman's shoulder, buzzed her hair, then abruptly stepped back. "You look terrific," he said. "Just terrific. Are you staying in the resort? Walk back with me."

"I can't."

"Caroline, you have to forgive me"

"Oh, I do, I do forgive you."

Markham sighed with relief, but Caroline heard something else. Her arm hooked around his and she guided him down a path away from both the resort and clubhouse.

"I want to be with you like we were before, I really do," she said. "Only, we need to be careful. They inserted an ethics clause in my contract. If my company discovered I slept with a client, I could lose my job."

"No one else needs to know." Even as he said it, Markham instinctively glanced at his watch. He wondered briefly when Kathryn would call; what would he do if she called right now?

"What do you think?" Caroline asked. They had halted in front of a low-slung cabin that looked from the outside like something early pioneers might have hewn out of the wilderness, provided they had an excellent sense of design.

"Very rustic," Markham said.

"It has three bedrooms, a full kitchen, living room, sauna, wet bar…" It also had a cedar deck that overlooked a pond and they were soon standing on it. "The company turned over all of the bungalows to its reps and left the resort to you guys. I think they wanted to make sure we got a break from each other."

"I wouldn't want a break from you," Markham said. His arm circled the woman's waist and pulled her close. He kissed her mouth. Caroline returned the kiss, but after a moment she broke it off.

"Come inside," she said and pulled him into the bungalow. She closed the door and stood with her back to Markham, gazing out the window at the empty path beyond. "My roommates will be back soon."

Markham rested his hands on the young woman's shoulder. "How soon?" he asked.

Caroline leaned backward against him.

"That time when we were together, I wasn't looking for a fling," Markham said. "When I met you in the bar and we started talking, I thought, hey, here's an interesting, intelligent woman. We seemed to have so much in common. We even have the same favorite song. What were the odds of that?"

"'Someone To Watch Over Me,'" Caroline said.

Markham was glad she remembered the title; he hadn't. His hands slid slowly down her bare arms, his fingertips gently caressed her flesh. She had goosebumps.

"I didn't think about us being together until we were on the elevator and I asked you what floor," Markham said.

"And I said five."

"And I was on eight."

"And the doors opened at five."

"And you didn't get off."

"Oh, God."

Caroline spun in Markham's arms and kissed him hard on the mouth. Markham was about to ask which of the three bedrooms belonged to her when Caroline pushed him away.

"Not now," she said. "Later. Tell me your room number and I'll meet you later."

Only later had been reserved for Kathryn.

"I—we'll see," Markham said.

The expression his remark put on Caroline's face frightened him. He actually took two steps backward.

"Why won't you tell me?" she said. "Are you seeing someone else? You are, aren't you? You're seeing someone else."

Just like that, Markham was tap-dancing on the edge of a scalpel. He knew Caroline would never confess to Susan that she was banging her husband. But tell her that someone else was sleeping with him—well, why wouldn't she? Women scorned, they need to stick together, don't they?

"Of course I'm not seeing anyone else," he said.

"You are."

The last time Markham had heard a voice sound that accusatory was years ago in an emergency room when a mother confronted the teenager who had just whacked her daughter with a car.

"Listen to me, Caroline."

"Damn you."

Caroline took three quick steps and pushed violently against Markham's chest. The momentum forced him backward. She pushed him again, but this time she didn't have a running start and he held his ground. When she attempted to pound his chest with clenched fists, he caught both of her wrists and pulled her close.

"Stop it," he snarled. "There are two women in my life. There's Susan and then there's you. No one else. Now stop it."

"I just want to be with you."

"I want to be with you, too. But I have a brother-in-law here who's been watching me and I have to be careful."

"A brother-in-law? At the resort?"

"Yes."

Caroline covered her mouth with her hand. "Oh, God, I'm so sorry," she said. "I thought—oh, God."

Markham wrapped her in his arms. "It's okay, it's all right," he told her.

"I thought…"

"I don't blame you."

Markham sighed. Another bullet dodged, he told himself. He stole a look at his watch. Kathryn was going to call at any moment and if Caroline saw them together... He had a thought that made him smile.

"Have dinner with me tonight," he said.

"What about your brother-in-law?"

"We'll ask him to join us."

Caroline seemed terrified by the prospect. "Your brother-in-law?"

"That's kind of a joke, we're not really related. But here's the thing, he's a doctor and I'm a doctor and you're a rep. Why wouldn't we get together for dinner? What could be more innocent? You can even make it a business dinner; give us your sales pitch." And pay the check, Markham thought but didn't say. "Afterwards"— Caroline brightened at the word—"we'll go to the casino. And then, who knows?"

"I always lose when I gamble," Caroline said.

"Not me."

★ ★ ★

Dr. Brookline was an old man and some on his staff—including Markham—actively pushed for his retirement. Even now he sat at a glass table on the resort's back patio, studying the handouts the pharmaceutical companies distributed because he was terrified that the advances in medicine would pass him by. Markham tried to avoid him, only Brookline saw him before he could escape.

"Good afternoon, Doctor," Brookline said. He gestured for Markham to sit. Markham sat.

"Good afternoon, Doctor," Markham replied.

"How have you been spending your day?"

"I just finished playing eighteen holes with..."

"I meant which seminars did you attend."

"Of course." Markham gave him a quick recap and Brookline nodded. He hummed a few times, but Markham didn't know if that meant he was pleased or not.

"You're a very good physician," Brookline said.

"Thank you, Doctor."

"There have been suggestions that it was time I retired."

"No."

"Some members of the board have indicated that they expect you to replace me."

"No one could replace you."

"Thank you for that, Doctor. Still, perhaps it is time. One is not getting any younger. The question is, are you ready to step into my shoes? I'll be frank, Doctor. There have been times when you have impressed me with, what shall I call it, your lack of judgment."

"Sir?"

"I am referring solely to your judgment outside the hospital. One hears rumors."

"I don't know how to respond to that, Doctor. I assure you that I have always tried to behave with the utmost caution in my personal affairs."

Brookline hummed some more.

"It is a discussion for a different time and place," he said. "We'll talk again when we return home."

With that, the old man went back to his handouts. Markham stood slowly. He knew when he had been dismissed.

"Sir," he said. "I am having dinner with Dr. Krueger and a rep from a pharmaceutical company. Perhaps you'd care to join us?"

"Thank you, Doctor, I already have plans. Dr. Krueger, you say? A steady hand. I am gratified to see you spending time with him."

Oh brother, Markham thought.

★ ★ ★

Markham couldn't believe it was possible. Caroline actually seemed to like the sniveling little creep. The way they connected, it was as if they had known each other for years. She laughed at Stephen's jokes and when she laughed, she would touch his arm and he would blush, actually blush, like a teenager on a first date. What comedy, Markham thought. Especially when they wrestled over the check. Caroline told Stephen that she would put it on her expense account, but if he really felt guilty about it, he could teach her how to play blackjack. "I'm terrible at cards," she said. Still, it gave Markham another idea.

Before they left the restaurant, Caroline stopped at the restroom. While they waited, Markham punched Stephen in the shoulder.

"You dawg," he said. "I didn't think you had it in you."

Stephen rubbed the spot where he had been hit. "What?"

"Like you don't know. 'Oh, please, Stephen. Can you teach me to play blackjack? I'm terrible at cards.'"

Stephen smiled sheepishly.

"You realize of course, that these reps have ethics clauses in their contracts," Markham said. "They're forbidden to sleep with clients."

"Really?" Stephen said. "Are you sure?"

Markham put his arm around Stephen's shoulder. "Don't worry about it. Rules are made to be broken, aren't they?"

★ ★ ★

Caroline and Stephen kept losing no matter how much they tried to help each other. Yet, neither of them seemed to care and for a moment, Markham felt a slight pang of jealousy. It disappeared when the cell phone attached to his belt started vibrating.

"Yes," he said into the phone.

"You are such a slut," Kathryn's voice said.

"Yes, this is Doctor Markham."

"You slept with her, didn't you?"

Markham slid his hand over the cell. "Excuse me," he told his companions and backed away from the blackjack table. Caroline watched him for a moment, then returned to her cards.

"What are you talking about?" Markham asked.

"I've been watching you. The way you touch her so casually when you're sure no one else will notice. It's so obvious."

"Is it?"

Kathryn laughed. "You should see your face," she said.

"What's wrong with my face?"

"From here it looks like you're experiencing an aneurysm."

"Where are you?" Markham spun in a slow, tight circle, searching for the woman.

"You'll see me soon enough," she said.

"Where?"

"The marina. There's a white cabin cruiser docked at the end of the middle pier. It's called *Miss Behavin'*. Meet me there in ten minutes. Don't let anyone see you. Promise."

Sex in a boat, that would be new, Markham thought. "I promise," he said.

"I have a sheer black negligee," Kathryn said. "Only it's such a warm night, I might not be wearing it by the time you arrive."

Markham deactivated the cell and reattached it to his belt. He returned to the blackjack table, stopping behind Caroline and Stephen. He placed a hand on each of their backs.

"Play my chips for me," he said. "I need to take care of something."

"You're leaving?" Caroline asked.

"No rest for the wicked," Markham said.

"Is it serious?" Stephen asked.

Markham wagged his hand. "I don't know yet. It could be. Caroline..." Markham wrapped his arms around her, hugged her tight and said loudly, "It was a pleasure meeting you. Let's do it again." Into her ear he whispered, "I'll call." He didn't hug Stephen, but Markham shook his hand and whispered into his ear as well. "Break the rules." He pulled back and looked him in the eye. "You know what I'm saying?"

"I know," Stephen said.

★ ★ ★

The marina lay on the far side of the resort. To reach it, Markham had to leave the casino, follow a long asphalt path to the resort itself, pass through the resort to the patio in back, pick up the asphalt path again, and follow it between the 11th and 12th holes of the golf course to the lake. He was tempted to run, only he didn't want to be tired and sweaty when he met Kathryn.

It's too bad about Caroline, he told himself. But if she slept with Stephen, it would afford him an excuse to break it off completely with her. If she complained, he'd tell her, "I used Stephen to see if you were faithful and you failed the test. Pity."

As he cut through the resort's opulent lobby, Markham was stopped by a man calling his name. Brookline was sitting in a stuffed forest-green chair and examining a medical journal, his black-rimming reading glasses perched on the tip of his nose.

"Calling it a night so soon, Dr. Markham?"

Why do these things keep happening to me? Markham's inner voice shouted.

"Good evening, Doctor," he said. "Yes. Early to bed, early to rise."

"I am gladdened to see it."

"I'm not much of a gambler. Besides, there's a seminar early tomorrow morning."

"Quite so," said Brookline. "I was thinking of turning in myself. But"—he gestured with his ancient hand toward the bar—"perhaps one might interest you in a nightcap."

"Thank you, Doctor. But I promised I'd call Susan."

"Of course." Brookline stood, yawned, stretched, and said, "I'll go up with you."

Markham and Dr. Brookline rode the elevator together—they were on the same floor. With his luck, Markham figured it couldn't be any other way. Brookline walked slowly along the corridor and Markham forced himself to keep pace. Markham came to his door first.

"Perhaps we can have breakfast together before the seminar," Brookline said.

"I'd like that very much, sir," Markham said.

"I'll call for you."

"I'll be waiting."

Markham opened his door, went into the room, closed his door, took his phone off the hook, sat on the wine-colored love seat, counted 210 seconds by his watch, opened the door, hung a Do Not Disturb sign on the knob, and scrambled down the emergency staircase.

★ ★ ★

Lake Vermilion shimmered in the moonlight. It had 1,200 miles of shoreline and 365 islands and Markham thought it would be great fun to take the boat and Kathryn and explore some of those islands. There were three piers jutting into the lake. Markham took the center one. Markham could hear only soft waves lapping gently at the hulls of the boats moored in the slips and the muffled sound of his footsteps on the wooden planks. He walked past fishing boats, pontoons, tour boats and an assortment of larger craft, some owned by guests, others for rent. At the end of the pier he found a white, 30-foot cabin cruiser. The name *Miss Behavin'* was stenciled on her bow and stern.

"Ahoy."

Kathryn's voice answered from the interior of the boat. "Dr. Markham?"

"Yes."

"Are you alone?"

"Yes."

"Did anyone see you? Does anyone know you're here?"

"Not a soul."

"Come aboard."

Markham stepped onto the deck of the boat and followed Kathryn's voice into the cabin. The moonlight that flooded through the narrow windows let him see the outline of furniture. Kathryn slid out of a shadow. She was naked.

"I like your outfit," Markham said, although he would have been happier if the lights were on and he could see more than her shape.

Kathryn stepped forward. Her face slipped from shadow to light and into shadow again. She was grinning. Once again Markham wished that the lights were on. He reached for her, rested his hands on the points of her bare shoulder. He liked the way her warm flesh felt beneath his fingertips. His arms slipped around her and he pulled her against him.

"I am so lucky that you sat in my row at the seminar," he said.

"Luck had nothing to do with it."

"What do you mean?"

"I have a message from your wife."

"My wife?"

"Susan says, 'You failed the test.'"

"What?"

Markham felt the 11-blade scalpel slice through the intercostal muscles between the fourth and fifth ribs and penetrate the left atrium of his heart. He found Kathryn's face in the darkness.

"Doctor," he said, as he collapsed to the floor.

But of course, she wasn't a doctor.

Scott Pearson

Scott Pearson, a lifelong Minnesotan, was first published in 1987 with "The Mailbox," a Minnesota Monthly Tamarack Award winner. Since then he has published a smattering of humor, poetry, short stories, and nonfiction, including The Mosquito Book, *which he coauthored with Scott Anderson (no relation) and Tony Dierckins. A Star Trek fan for thirty-five years, Scott has had three Trek stories published by Simon & Schuster, most recently "Among the Clouds" in* The Sky's the Limit, *a Star Trek: The Next Generation anthology. Scott makes his living as an editor for Zenith Press, a military history publisher in St. Paul, and X-comm, a regional history publisher in Duluth. He has edited such books as* Tales from a Tin Can: The USS Dale from Pearl Harbor to Tokyo Bay, *which received a starred review in* Publishers Weekly, *and* Will To Murder: The True Story Behind the Crimes & Trials Surrounding the Glensheen Killings, *which was featured in Dominick Dunne's* Power, Privilege, and Justice *series on CourtTV. "Out of the Jacuzzi, Into the Sauna" is Scott's first mystery story. He lives in St. Paul with his wife, Sandra, and daughter, Ella. Please visit him on the web at* **www.yeahsure.net.**

Out of the Jacuzzi, Into the Sauna

Scott Pearson

I'm taking off my clothes," Kate said. Holding her damp white shirt away from her skin, she flopped it around to try to cool off, then started unbuttoning.

Bill looked up and dragged an arm across his forehead to stop the sweat from running into his eyes. His graying hair was plastered across his head, and his blue polo shirt was soggy and hanging on his shoulders. "I don't think that's a good idea."

"First off, I never thought I'd hear my husband say that. Second, we're in a sauna."

"Locked in a sauna. There's a difference."

She stopped unbuttoning. "That's all you've got to say? How about the guy with the gun doesn't deserve to see me topless?"

That's when the door opened.

★ ★ ★

Things had first gone wrong the day before when Kate called to confirm check-in time at Great Lakes Lodges. She and Bill had been leaning against the side of their car at a scenic overlook on the North Shore of Lake Superior. It was the eighth of September, and a cool breeze blew in off the water, warning of fall as the waves crashed on the rocky shore. Sea gulls, talking among themselves, glided by just a few feet above Bill and Kate, hoping for a handout. The dark lake was so large that the far off Wisconsin shore was easy to miss. Turning to the northeast, Wisconsin faded away altogether, and the lake became an ocean. Split Rock Lighthouse, watching over the lake from a rock bluff further up the Minnesota shore, gave the effect of being on the coast of Maine.

Bill glanced at his watch. "Let's get going. I hear a Jacuzzi calling."

"Check-in's not until four." Kate brushed her long brown hair—she liked to call the gray strands "highlights"—out of her eyes, but another gust of wind whipped it right back.

"I thought it was at three."

"No, four."

"Three."

"Four."

"Three."

"Four." She pulled the cell phone out of her jacket pocket, scrolled down to the number, and hit the call button. Someone picked up before the second ring.

"Dammit, Jack, I just told you to leave this line open."

"First off, this isn't 'Dammit Jack,' this is 'Go to hell Kate.' Second, when's check-in?"

"Oh—I'm very sorry, I'm having trouble with a new employee using the outside line. Again, I apologize. Check-in is at four p.m., ma'am."

"The apology was all right, but you lost me at 'ma'am.' Thanks." Kate dropped the phone back into her pocket and squinted at Bill. "Four."

Bill squinted back, accentuating his laugh lines. "Go to hell, Kate."

"Very funny. Keep in mind the new guy ties up the phone while seducing all the hot older women that stay there."

"That's a problem."

"Don't worry." She patted his belly. "I'm spoken for."

Bill shook his head. "I was talking about check-in. Now we have some time to kill."

"That's going to cost you."

He smiled and looked back down to the lake just as a large wave broke, sending a spray all the way up to their shoes. "Twenty years ago we'd be down on those rocks, not up here leaning on the car."

She smiled back. "Twenty years ago we never would've gotten out of the car."

"Twenty years ago we had a bigger car."

They both turned and looked at their little Scion hatchback. "Good point." She looked back toward the shore. "Let's go down to the rocks, goat boy."

"That's goat man, if you please."

★ ★ ★

"The turn should be any moment now," Kate said. They'd come down the North Shore, hugging the big lake as they continued south past Beaver Bay, through the Silver Creek Cliff Tunnel, and then on through Two Harbors. Kate had sent their eighteen-year-old, Max, a cell phone picture she'd taken on the rocky beach, then called to tell him about it. He'd accused her of using the picture as an excuse to check on him, she'd feigned denial, and then he'd laughed at her as he said goodbye. Just south of the city, Kate pointed ahead to their left. "There, where that car is."

A silver sports wagon sat at the end of the driveway without a signal on, but just as Bill started turning in, it squealed out in front of them. Bill slammed the breaks and laid on the horn, killing the engine as they skidded to a stop just before hitting the passenger side of the wagon. They got a good look at its tinted windows, then watched it race down the road ahead of them toward Duluth.

"What was that about?" Kate had her hands on the dashboard and forced herself to exhale as she turned toward Bill. She lifted one hand to push a lock of damp hair out of her eyes.

Bill clenched the wheel with one hand and finally took the other off the horn. "Damn people in their Beemers think they own the road."

"You okay?" She put a hand on his leg.

"Yeah. You?" He turned toward her, his look softening.

"Just startled." She adjusted her shoulder belt. "Might have a bruise."

He nodded. "Well, let's get out of the road." Glancing left and right as he restarted the car, he crossed into the driveway.

Kate looked around as she rubbed her right shoulder. The road to the lodge was surrounded by evergreens, birch, and poplar. She opened her window, letting in the late summer breeze, filling the car with the smell of pine. The road curved away from the lake, surrounding the car in the forest before it turned back, dramatically revealing the rustic main lodge and the backdrop of Lake Superior.

Kate sighed happily. "This is nice."

"If you like this sort of thing," Bill mumbled as he parked the car in front of the lodge.

"Come on, you're just cranky about that lunatic who cut us off."

"You're right. I'll relax once I hit the bubbles."

"Champagne or Jacuzzi?"

"Preferably both."

They went inside and were greeted on the left by a black bear carved out of a log and on their right by a moose head hanging on the wall. A small fire was burning in a stone fireplace in the center of the large lobby. Quiet music played in the background, woodwinds and acoustic guitar mixed with the sounds of running water and gentle breezes. Walking across an inlaid-tile map of Lake Superior, they approached the front desk, where a perfectly coiffed man in his thirties awaited as he adjusted his blue suit coat and yellow tie.

"Good afternoon, welcome to Great Lakes Lodges. I'm Stephan—how may I help you today?" Kate recognized the voice from her phone call an hour ago; in person it was just as smooth and over-arranged as his hair.

"Well," said Bill. "You can let the owner of the BMW sports wagon know that although the five series doesn't come with manners, I'm fairly certain it has turn signals."

"Excuse me?" Stephan looked back and forth between Bill and Kate, eyebrows raised in apparent confusion.

"One of your guests almost ran us off the road," Kate said. She could tell by Stephan's expression he recognized her voice as well.

"I'm sorry—this is a little awkward for me." The man looked around to see if anyone might overhear. Kate made a show of checking the lobby as well, keeping a close eye on the moose head. "That wasn't a guest." He leaned forward. Kate gave the carved bear a suspicious glance. "The BMW belongs to Magda Burgraff, the manager," he whispered. "She's been acting a little strange since Jack started working here."

"Dammit Jack, you mean?" Kate also leaned forward, putting her elbows on the desk and her chin in her hands. "Come on, dish it up. Is he blackmailing her? She having a fling with him? Both?"

Stephan straightened up and shook his head. "You didn't hear that from me. She is married after all."

"That doesn't stop some people. I have a cousin who—"

Bill coughed and gave her a look.

She looked back at him, blinking her eyes innocently. "Lozenge?"

Bill turned back to Stephan. "Sorry, my wife can't help teasing people. Can we just check in, please?"

"Certainly, sir." Stephan gave them a look like a child sharing a secret. "But to be honest—the way she tore out of here, I don't think Mrs. Burgraff is ever coming back."

★ ★ ★

By the time they took the short drive to their cabin, it was already four-thirty. The cabin, almost surrounded by trees on a small point jutting into the lake, had a beautiful view of the water. They were almost there when Bill had to slam on the brakes as a man burst from a path in the woods and sprinted across the road toward the main lodge.

"What is it with this place?" said Bill as he eased the car ahead the last several yards and parked in front of the cabin.

"Don't get riled." Kate rolled up her window. "Sure, we've had a couple of bumps in the road—"

"Almost literally," Bill interjected.

"—but now we're at our cabin," Kate continued, ignoring the interruption. "Everything will be fine now."

They got out of the car and were welcomed by the sound of a vacuum cleaner.

"It's over a half hour after check-in and they're still cleaning?" Bill shook his head. "I just want the relaxing to start."

They grabbed their luggage and cooler and went in through the open door of the cabin. The hallway, bathroom, and kitchen had a linoleum floor, but the living room and bedroom had a nice thick carpet. A young woman—her name tag said Anna—waved at them as she turned off the vacuum. "Sorry, I just have the vacuuming to finish up."

Bill put down a suitcase. "How much longer?"

"About fifteen minutes, sir."

He sighed. "I'm going to fill the tub." He headed back to the bathroom, and Kate winked as he passed her. Bill rolled his eyes and kept walking.

She turned back to Anna. "Rough day?"

"Yeah, I had to clean Mrs. Burgraff's room, and I've been running late ever since."

Kate folded her arms. Down the hall, she could hear water splashing. "Stephan told us she wasn't coming back. Did she quit?"

"I don't know—she wasn't even there. Jack packed her stuff in her car and told me to clean up after him. I did see her drive off a little later. "

Kate thought, *I was only kidding, but maybe Dammit Jack is having an affair with the boss.* "Did he pack any of his stuff in the car?"

"No, ma'am." Anna suddenly looked nervous. "But Stephan told me not to gossip about Jack and Mrs. Burgraff."

Kate nodded. *Something is definitely going on between them—or it's over, if he isn't leaving with her.* But then he would've had no business packing up her office. "What's his job?"

Before she got an answer a clanging sound followed by a broadside of swearing erupted over the sound of running water. She hurried down the hallway and peaked into the large bathroom. Bill sat on the edge of a Jacuzzi made for two, his shoulders slumped.

"What happened?" Kate said.

"I started the water and grabbed a towel from the shelf. Then I saw all that crud coming out of the faucet." Kate leaned forward and saw several clots of rust floating in the water. As more water splashed into the tub, the clots tumbled around as if alive.

She wrinkled her nose as she reached down to turn the water off. "Eeewww."

"That's what I'm saying. I hung the towel on the rack so I could drain the water, but the rack fell off the wall." He held up the rack in his hand.

"I'm sorry, sir," Anna said. "Jack was supposed to take care of that." She turned to Kate with an embarrassed look. "He's the maintenance man."

Bill frowned. "Dammit, Jack."

★ ★ ★

While Anna cleaned up the Jacuzzi, Kate had decided to take a swim in the pool, and maybe spend a little time in the sauna as well. Bill was too pouty to join her, so he stayed at the cabin to read. Kate checked herself out in the bedroom mirror, then pulled her robe closed over her new one-piece swimsuit. She felt pretty good about it, but not quite good enough to flaunt it, and the late afternoon walk would be a bit chilly. She headed out the door and down a paved path to the main lodge, her flip-flops slapping the asphalt.

As she made her way along the wooded path, she could hear a blue jay shriek in the branches above her, the insistent chirp of a chipmunk in the bushes, and the gentle lapping of the lake on the beach. At a break in the trees she paused to enjoy the view. Across a wide beach of small smooth stones, the lake, dotted with seagulls, swelled and rolled like some giant animal settling into its bed. A group of sailboats, small in the distance, cruised toward the Duluth port, full sails billowing under a stiff breeze.

Kate took a deep breath of the lake air, shivered a bit, then continued along the path, which led to a side door on the south wing of the lodge. Next to the door was a large ice chest, like the kind outside of gas stations. Maybe she'd grab a bag of ice on her way back to the cabin. Going into the lodge, Kate walked down a

65

hallway that ran alongside the pool room, but the tall windows all along the left had their shades down. She spotted a door ahead to the left, where the hall took a turn to the right toward the lobby. Just as she reached the door, a man came out and she caught a glimpse of a large pool and, on the other side of it, a steaming, bubbling hot tub. She was surprised to see no one in the water and looked forward to having the pool to herself. But then the man closed the door and locked it behind him. All that remained was the smell of chlorine in the air.

Glancing up at him, she recognized the sprinter from the woods. He looked to be in his late thirties. He was handsome in a rough and craggy kind of way, but vaguely menacing like a hitchhiker you'd pass on a country back road. He had the smell of cigarettes on him, even though he wasn't smoking.

"I was hoping to take a swim," she said.

"Sorry, ma'am, the pool's closed for maintenance."

She looked up at rough and smoky again. "Jack, I assume?"

His eyes widened in surprise for a moment, then narrowed. "Do I know you?"

"No, you haven't had the pleasure." She folded her arms. "The pool looked fine to me."

"Sure, it looks fine. But the water's off. I had to add some chemicals. Maybe it'll be ready tomorrow."

"Just a sauna, then."

"No. I have to close the whole room."

Kate shook her head. "Dammit, Jack, I was really looking forward to this."

He looked surprised again, then frowned before walking away without another word, heading down the hall to the lobby.

"All right, tomorrow then," she called after him. "You'll still be here, right?" He ignored her. With a smile, she started back to the cabin.

★ ★ ★

Bill was still in the Jacuzzi when she got back, steam billowing out of the open bathroom door. "Back so soon?" he said when she stepped into the room and let her robe fall to the floor. He looked her up and down. "You're not wet."

"You're a clever man. In a better mood?"

"I am now."

"You like my suit?"

"Yes, I do. But I'd like it more on the floor with your robe."

"Why, sir, you are so forward." She teasingly wriggled out of her suit and got into the water, snuggling into Bill as he put an arm around her.

"So what happened?"

"The pool was closed. And I met Dammit Jack. I wasn't impressed."

"He's not the young Lothario that seduced Mrs. Burgraff?"

"First off, he's not so young. Second, he's kind of creepy. I can't imagine what she sees in him."

"Maybe Mr. Burgraff is older and creepier."

"Or maybe something else is going on."

"Like what?"

"I don't know. I need more clues."

"Not another imaginary mystery."

"Hey, I'm just having fun. But get this—he was the guy that ran across the road in front of us."

"So he's a jaywalker." Bill settled a little deeper in the water. "How about we do something else for a while?"

"Like what?"

He grabbed her under the water.

"You are forward. Just be careful of my sore shoulder."

"Don't worry, I'm not going near your shoulder."

★ ★ ★

The Arrowhead Room, Great Lakes Lodges' restaurant and bar, was decorated with local flair, from Ojibwe Indian artifacts to a model of the Edmund Fitzgerald to an HO scale Duluth, Missabe & Iron Range Railway train that ran around the room on a shelf near the ceiling. Bill and Kate walked up to the buffet, which, around 7:30, had no line. Still, the restaurant was nearly full, and the din of talking and clinking of silverware gave them a sense of privacy as they stood close together beside the table of prepared entrées and side dishes.

"I don't like buffets." Kate scooped up some broiled salmon. "The food always has that special quality of being both overcooked and tepid."

"I'm too hungry to wait to order." Bill grabbed a steak with some tongs.

"We did work up an appetite, didn't we?"

"And a bit of a slosh in the Jacuzzi. Or should I say out of the Jacuzzi?"

Kate added some garlic mashed potatoes to her plate. "That's what mops are for."

"Look at this." Bill pointed at some framed pictures on the wall showing various events that the Lodge had hosted. In one, a book release party, a willowy young woman stood next to the author, who held up a copy of his book. Her shoulder-length auburn hair stood out from her black cocktail dress, which showed a lot of leg, and a simple but elegant necklace hung down her low-cut neckline.

"Holy crap," said Kate as she read a small notecard on the wall beneath the picture. "The woman with the gams is Magda Burgraff."

"Not quite the matron I expected from her name."

"Even less likely she'd be interested in Dammit Jack."

Bill leaned in closer. "You have a point there."

Kate put a hand on his chest and pushed him back. "You don't need to look that closely."

"I was just thinking you have the curves that would really make that dress work."

"Nice recovery."

"I thought so."

"But I still say there's something hinky going on."

Before Bill could respond, Stephan appeared at their side. "Excuse me," he whispered. "Could I please speak to both of you in the lobby?"

"Now what?" Bill said. "We're in the middle of the buffet."

"Please, it's important."

Bill looked at Kate, but she had her usual curious twinkle in her eyes. He sighed and set down his plate. They followed Stephan into the lobby, stopping in front of the large stone fireplace in the center of the room. Three big logs snapped and popped as they blazed away. Stephan gave one of his conspiratorial glances around the room. Kate once again stared down the wooden bear and moose head.

"Mr. Burgraff just called. His wife never arrived in Duluth after she left here this afternoon."

Bill gave Kate a sideways glance. "She probably stopped at a friend's house."

Kate shook her head with an I-told-you-so look on her face, then turned back to Stephan. "Why tell us?"

"Because you saw her last, as far as I know. If she's declared a missing person, the police will want to talk to you."

"First off, we only glimpsed her car. Second, why don't you ask Dammit Jack when he last saw her?"

Stephan almost smirked. "Why would I do that?"

"Because we heard he packed her things. So either he talked to her last and she asked him to, or he didn't talk to her and he shouldn't have been doing it. Either way, he's involved."

"Well, that's a bit personal. I don't think you should be spreading rumors about—"

Bill straightened up. "It's time for you to stop talking, Steve."

Stephan looked shocked. "My name is—"

"I know what you call yourself, but I'd wager good money that's not what your mother named you." Bill paused a moment, but Stephan just clenched his jaw. "That's what I thought. Okay— since you dragged us into this, you don't get to turn around and call my wife a liar, understand? So we're going back to our cabin now to enjoy ourselves, despite your missing manager and malcontent maintenance man. And, to make up for all the trouble we've been having since before we even arrived, you're going to send us a couple of your best entrées, a bottle of big red wine, and a selection of your finest desserts, all on the house. Do I make myself clear? Steve?"

Stephan's throat moved as though he were swallowing a golf ball, then his professional smile came back. "Yes, sir. Of course, sir. Sorry for the interruption."

Bill nodded. "All right then." He stared at Stephan until Stephan headed back into the Arrowhead Room.

Kate watched Stephan go, then turned back to Bill. "Wow."

Bill smiled a bit as he rolled his head around to loosen up. "Yeah, that was pretty good, wasn't it?"

"It was great." Kate folded Bill's arm through hers as they headed away from the fireplace, down the corridor to the side exit. After a moment she looked up at him. "Missing manager and malcontent maintenance man?"

"You mock my alliteration?"

"Perhaps I partake of a pinch of parody of your patter."

They laughed, leaning into each other as they walked. As they approached the door to the pool room, Jack came out, scowled at them, and locked the door. Kate yanked on Bill's arm as Jack stomped toward them.

"That's Mr. Sunshine," Kate said.

As Jack neared them, Bill said, "How's your boss?"

Jack stopped short and looked Bill up and down, as if assessing his strength. Bill, although in good enough shape for a man of forty-seven, was no fighter, and Kate felt afraid of Jack for the first time. But Bill, apparently energized by his confrontation with Stephan (though Kate thought she could probably take Stephan), stood up straighter as if ready to go a couple rounds with the younger maintenance man. Jack finally just smirked and walked around them toward the lobby.

"How should I know?" he tossed back over his shoulder. "She took off."

"Here's the interesting thing," Bill said. Jack kept walking. "When we got here this afternoon, Stephan told us she's been acting strangely since you were hired."

That brought Jack to a stop. He spun around with a glare, then tried to act casual with a shrug of his shoulders. "Don't know what he's talking about."

"I think you do." Bill actually took a step closer to Jack.

Kate jumped in to distract Jack from Bill. "He also told Anna not to gossip about the two of you."

Jack turned toward her. After a moment he turned his back on them and continued down the hall.

Kate waited until Jack disappeared around a corner then gave Bill a push on the shoulder. "What's gotten into you?" She still felt a little afraid of how the two men had postured. "Next thing I know you're going to get a tattoo and fight a bare-knuckle cage match."

"That isn't going to happen." Bill's shoulders slouched. "That scared the hell out of me. I didn't dare blink, though." He took a few deep breaths and released them. "I just couldn't help myself once I knew he was involved with her."

"How do you know that?"

Bill looked down the hall in the direction Jack had gone. "Dammit Jack had a BMW key on his key chain. I spotted the logo."

★ ★ ★

"So what do you think?" Kate said as she settled into their morning Jacuzzi.

Bill already relaxed in the bubbling water, his eyes closed.

"I think things are going much better." They had had a nice dinner the night before, courtesy of Stephan, and an evening of further diversions had helped them ignore the intrigue of the manager and the maintenance man.

Kate poked Bill underwater with her foot. "I meant what do you think's going on with Dammit Jack and Gams McBurgraff?"

Bill shrugged. "Could be nothing. Maybe she just gave him the key when she asked him to pack her things."

"But then where is she? Why did she take off without telling anyone?"

He opened his eyes. "She's leaving her husband. With Jack or someone else. Or no one else. People do that sometimes, just up and leave."

"Don't get any ideas."

"Don't worry, I'm staying right here. The water's perfect."

"Very funny." She poked him underwater again. "How about this... Jack stole the car, stashed it down the road a ways, then hoofed it back to the Lodge. Which is when he ran in front of us."

"But why do that?" Bill closed his eyes again, looking like he could fall asleep.

After a moment Kate said, "He was waiting at the end of the driveway for someone to come by. Waiting to squeal out in front of them to make sure he was noticed."

Bill opened one eye. "To make sure her car was noticed."

"Exactly. He tells everyone she's leaving, packs the car, then creates witnesses to 'her' rushing off."

His other eye opened. "And we're back to where is Gams, and why is Jack covering up that she's missing."

"That's the mystery, isn't it?"

"Yes, Inspector."

★ ★ ★

After they showered and dressed, they went down to the Arrowhead Room for breakfast. Entering through the side door, they saw that the pool was still locked up. Kate shook her head as they walked by. Once they were seated in the restaurant, they ordered off the menu, and lingered over their after-breakfast espressos.

Bill watched the DM&IR train roll by over their heads and slouched in his chair. "So what'll we do today? Take a hike by the lake? Maybe a picnic lunch?"

"Sounds good. We could hike up that trail we saw Dammit Jack come from."

Bill frowned. "You really are taking this seriously."

"I am." She leaned forward and took another sip of espresso. "If we found Gams's abandoned car, I bet she could be declared a missing person. Then we could tell the police about the key and get them to question Dammit Jack."

Coming out of his slouch, Bill rested his chin on one hand, elbow on the table. "And what if we don't find the car? It's kind of fun playing detective, but this is supposed to be a vacation. I don't want to—"

"But you admit it's suspicious no one has seen her. And you spotted Jack's BMW key yourself."

"Still, for all we know, she's at home with her husband right now."

Kate furrowed her brow. "You're right. Come on, let's ask Stephan." She didn't wait for an answer, instead just pushed out her chair and took a few steps away from the table. Looking back over her shoulder, she said, "You coming?"

Bill rolled his eyes. "Yes, Inspector."

After the short walk out of the restaurant and across the lobby, they found Stephan behind the front desk. Seeing them approach, he smiled like someone trying to look strong while getting a sliver extracted.

Kate didn't let that stop her. "Have you heard anything from the Burgraffs?"

Stephan adjusted his gray suit coat and straightened his blue tie. "I was under the impression you didn't want me to bother you about that again. Last night—"

"Just answer the question, Steve," said Bill.

After glaring a moment at Bill, Stephan said, "Mr. Burgraff has not heard from his wife. He has reported it to the police. And I gave your names to them."

"Fine," said Kate. "We look forward to talking to them." She headed out of the lobby, down the hall to the side door, with Bill following behind her.

As they passed the pool, Bill pointed at the shuttered windows. "Still not open."

★ ★ ★

Kate didn't say another word until they were back in the cabin. "We're going up that path. Stephan would've said something if the police had found her car. Maybe it's still up there."

"Listen, Inspector—"

Kate folded her arms across her chest. "Stop calling me that. It's not funny."

He held his hands up in surrender. "Fine. But let's at least bring a picnic lunch so I can pretend we're having a normal vacation."

"You wouldn't have married me if you wanted normal."

"Good point."

Kate went into the kitchen and looked in the refrigerator. "I think we've got enough stuff for a picnic. Why don't you make some sandwiches? I'll go back to the lodge and get some ice for the cooler. I forgot to grab some last night."

"Okay. Leave me the cell, though. I want to call Max."

She took the phone out of her jacket pocket and tossed it to Bill. "Say 'hi' for me."

"I will."

Heading out the door, she followed the path as it curved to the right into the woods, keeping roughly an even distance from the shore of the lake as it led her off the point and to the lodge. She walked briskly, not paying attention to the natural surroundings. Leaving the woods, she jogged the remaining yards to the ice chest by the side entrance. She saw the padlock on the chest's thick silver door, then the note taped to the top of the chest: "Out of order."

"Dammit, Jack." First the pool, now this. She turned toward the side door, but stopped when the ice chest rumbled to life. Turning back, she leaned over to place her hand on the silver door. Through the insulation she could feel an undeniable chill. There was nothing wrong with the ice chest. Then something shiny on the ground caught her eye. She knelt down and retrieved a necklace from the grass in front of the chest—the necklace she had seen dangling down Mrs. Burgraff's low-cut dress in the picture in the Arrowhead Room.

She straightened her back, although she remained kneeling. She looked from the necklace in her hand to the large, rumbling ice chest. Just what's locked in there? she wondered. She grabbed in her pocket for the phone, but it was back at the cabin with Bill. Taking the necklace with her, she hurried inside, running down the hall toward the lobby.

There was no one at the front desk when she got there. She reached over to grab the phone. That's when Stephan appeared from the office behind the desk.

"May I help you?" He squinted at her hand on the receiver.

Yanking her hand back, she held up the necklace in her other hand. "I think we should call the police. I just found this outside."

Stephan's eyes widened as he recognized the necklace. He glanced around for other guests. "Come back here, we'll use the office phone."

She went behind the front desk, following him into the small office. He closed the door behind her as she entered. Kate hesitated beside a rolltop desk with a phone on it. "Should I call, or do you want to?"

"Why don't you call your husband first, so he can come down here too?" Stephan said from behind her.

Turning around, Kate said, "Call the police first, then . . ." She trailed off when she saw that Stephan had a gun in his hand. It all came to her then. It was Stephan who had told them that the BMW was Burgraff's. Who told them she'd been acting strangely, that he thought she wasn't coming back, that they had been the last to see her. He had even given their names to the police, all so they would report they had seen her leave the lodge. She had been so focused on Dammit Jack she hadn't realized how much Stephan had been maneuvering them.

"Get your husband." Stephan's voice wavered as he spoke; so did the gun as his hand trembled. "Just ask him to meet you here, nothing else."

Kate picked up the receiver without taking her eyes from the gun. She knew nothing about guns, but it looked real and big. As she put the receiver to her ear, she said, "I don't know how." He told her the extension, which she punched in. When Bill answered she hesitated, then said, "Hey, could you come down to the lobby? I—" Stephan held the gun higher, a warning about what she said next. "I want to show you something."

She hung up. "He'll be right here."

Stephan nodded. It seemed to take an hour for Bill to arrive, but she finally heard him at the front desk. "Hello? Kate?"

Stephan opened the door a bit. "Back in the office, sir. We're just about to call the police."

Kate wanted to cry out, to keep Bill from coming into the office, but Stephan kept his eyes and the gun on her. She clenched her hands into fists as Bill entered the doorway. Stephan stepped aside, dropping his arm out of view for a second. Before Kate could think of anything to do, Bill was by her side, and they were both looking at the gun, which was raised again.

"Do you have your cell phone?" Stephan said. Bill nodded. "Give it to me. Carefully." Bill handed it over. Stephan dialed then put it to his ear. "Meet me in the pool room. There's another problem." He dropped the phone into his jacket pocket.

Jack, thought Kate. He's still a part of this. He did drive the BMW and pack the office. And he had kept calling Stephan on the outside line—probably for instructions—that's how he got to be Dammit Jack. She wondered why Stephan had used their cell, but then he gestured with the gun.

"We're leaving now. If we meet any other guests, don't say a word."

As Bill took her hand and they went out the door and around the front desk, Kate doubted Stephan would shoot them in front of witnesses; still, she wasn't about to call his bluff. But they met no one as they walked to the pool room; the other guests were out enjoying the day. Stephan openly held the gun on them as he unlocked the door to the pool with his other hand. Opening the door wide, he gestured them in with the gun.

They went inside, the smell of chlorine strong, but there was another aroma in the air that Kate didn't immediately identify. As Stephan locked the door behind them, she noticed a large spot on the tile beside the pool which was cleaner than its surroundings. Then she recognized the other smell—bleach. In her mind she saw the attractive young Magda Burgraff lying beside the pool, blood swelling around her head. Shots would have been heard; Stephan must have bludgeoned her with something. Then Jack closed the room for "maintenance," cleaned the blood with bleach, dumped extra chlorine into the tainted pool. She forced herself to look away from the clean spot.

"Get in the sauna." Stephan pronounced it *saw-na*.

"It's pronounced with an *ow*." Her nerves had gotten the better of her. All the shades were still down, and the room had already been the scene of one murder. "As in, 'Ow, it's hot in here.'"

"Shut up," Stephan said.

"It's Finnish, you know. This is Minnesota, not California."

"Just get in there!"

Kate risked a glance at Bill, and he gave her a look—sympathetic, but warning her to stop blathering. Holding hands, they did what they were told and went into the sauna. Although the pool had been closed since yesterday, the sauna had been left on, and it was at least 120 degrees inside.

"It'll do wonders for my pores," Kate said. As soon as they were both in, the door slammed shut behind them. They heard a clanging sound as something was jammed against the door from the outside.

"Don't annoy the guy with the gun," Bill said as he grabbed the thermostat beside the door and turned it off. "He already didn't like us."

"He liked me."

"Not anymore."

"Sorry. I'm just scared."

The edge left his voice as they hugged. "I know. Me too." They held on for a long time, but even in their situation the heat eventually drove them to step back.

After a few minutes, Kate said, "Should we try to break out of here?"

Bill had his ear as close to the door as he could stand, the wood too hot to touch. "No. I think he's still out there waiting for Jack."

They stood quietly for several more minutes. Dark stains appeared under Bill's arms, and Kate felt her shirt clinging to her back. Although they had turned off the heat, the room wasn't cooling down much. "I'm taking off my clothes," she said.

★ ★ ★

When the door opened, Bill and Kate, her shirt still unbuttoned, backed away to the far wall. They stopped next to the heater, its top covered with rocks. Jack leaned in and looked from Kate to Bill and quickly back at Kate. "Get out here." He disappeared, but left the door open. Kate and Bill moved toward the welcome cool air, but nervous about leaving the relative safety of the sauna.

As they stepped out, Bill reached for Kate's hand, but she wrapped her arm around his back instead. He responded in kind and pulled her close as they came to a stop in front of Stephan and Jack. Stephan had the gun on them, his breathing was quick and shallow.

"Tie their hands behind their backs," Stephan said. His usually perfect hair laid on his head like wet shag.

Jack frowned, glancing at the gun, and walked to the pool. He pulled a knife from a belt sheath and cut the rope hanging between the shallow and deep end, then walked around the pool to cut away the other end of the rope.

"Move apart." Stephan motioned with the gun. Instead, Bill and Kate wrapped their arms around each other in a desperate hug. Stephan swallowed, another golf ball moving through his neck. Jack hesitated as he approached with the dripping rope.

"Step apart or I'll shoot you both right now." The threat crackled in the air like static, but Bill and Kate couldn't seem to let go of each other.

"Not here," said Jack. He took a step toward Stephan. "We'll get caught."

"You're the idiot who dropped the necklace."

"If you hadn't killed her, we—"

"I told you, that was an accident. She was going to skip on both of us."

Jack shook his head. "That's what you keep saying." He approached Kate and Bill, lifting his knife. Kate flinched, but Jack only cut off a shorter piece of rope.

She let out a breath, then whispered something she'd figured out. "He told us about you and Magda so we'd tell the police."

Jack squinted at her as he cut off another short section, letting the long piece fall to the tiled floor. He slipped the knife back into its sheath.

"What's she saying?" Stephan said. "Shut her up."

Jack gestured at Bill. "You first." But his eyes stayed glued on Kate.

"You hid her body. Packed her office. Moved her car."

"I said shut her up! Dammit, Jack, get them tied."

Jack looked over his shoulder at Stephan. "Promise me half the money first."

"What?" Stephan forced a laugh. "You'll get what we agreed on."

"I should get half. I'm doing all the work."

"You? I helped Magda skim for years. I earned my share long before you bounced into her bed. You get what you deserve."

"What's that—a frame up?" He waved his hands around. "It's all on me, you made sure of that."

Stephan glared at Jack for a few more seconds, then shrugged. "All right, fifty-fifty. Now just tie them up so we can get out of here."

Jack turned back to them with a smile. He held up the rope in one hand, patted the knife with the other. "Don't make me cut you apart." Kate tensed and hugged Bill even harder. As if she'd squeezed it out of him, Bill blurted, "He called you on our cell."

Kate got it as Jack's smile faded. "Your number's on our phone." It would lead the police to him.

Jack turned and took a step toward Stephan, dropping the rope. "Give me that phone."

Stephan also stepped forward, the gun shaking. "Forget the phone!"

Jack lunged at him.

Stephan swung the gun toward Jack. Jack grabbed his arm. The gun waved toward Kate and Bill. They jumped aside as a shot rang out. Floor tiles shattered.

Everyone froze. The pool murmured in the background. The echo of the shot hung in the humid air.

Then Stephan and Jack struggled again. Stephan got the gun between them but their arms tangled. Another shot, muffled by close bodies. A wet intake of breath.

Stephan, arms clamped to his gut, tumbled to the floor. The gun skittered across the tile past Bill. Bill and Jack both went for the gun. Bill got there first, diving for it. Jack loomed behind him, drawing his knife.

But as Jack hurried by Kate, she swung a roundhouse punch into his jaw. With a distinct crack, Jack went down like a tree. He slammed into the floor without even putting his arms out. Kate yelped as a hot sauna rock flew from her red palm. It bounced once off the tile with the clack of a billiard ball, then splashed into the pool.

Bill, dropping the gun, hurried back to her, and they were in each others arms again, Kate still flapping her burned hand. She couldn't stop smiling at Bill, and without having noticed it happening, her face was covered in tears.

Then they heard shouting from outside, the door rattling, keys jangling, and several employees rushed into the room. A couple of them went to check on Jack and Stephan.

"I'm calling nine-one-one," someone said.

A different voice said, "What happened?"

Bill said, "They were stealing from the lodge. Them and Magda."

"I think she's dead," added Kate. "Stuffed in the ice chest."

"No way." That was Anna. "You guys all right?"

"Just a burn," Kate said. Bill blew on her hand.

They were led to the lobby and settled onto a couch in front of the fireplace. Anna brought a first-aid kit and gave Kate a cold pack. Time bounced by in disjointed scenes. Someone gave them coffee. An EMT looked at Kate's hand. They overheard the coroner saying Magda Burgraff's legs were broken to stuff her into the ice chest. A uniformed officer spoke with them briefly. They saw Jack led out in handcuffs, his jaw swollen. Stephan was rolled by on a gurney by EMTs. An officer walked alongside.

"He went crazy and shot me," he told them between gasps of pain. "He killed her too. Everything was just fine until she hired him. I told her not to!"

After a few minutes, Kate said, "Good job about the cell phone. I'll make you a detective yet."

"Thanks."

"So did you notice what Jack did back there?"

80

"The way he hit the bricks after you tagged him with that rock?"

"That kicked ass, but no. I meant when he got us out of the sauna. He checked out my unbuttoned shirt—a complete double take. I'm forty-six, but I'm still hot."

"We were in a sauna."

"Very funny. And to think I was going to call you brave for going for the gun."

A detective came towards them with more coffee.

"So," said Bill. "This is some vacation."

"Yeah," Kate said. "First off, they really need to rethink their hiring practices. Second, we should come back here for fall colors. This is getting fun."

Pat Dennis

Pat Dennis is the author of the regional bestseller, Hotdish to Die For, *a collection of six mystery short stories and 18 hotdish recipes where the weapon of choice is often hotdish. Her fiction and humor have been published in* Minnesota Monthly, Woman's World, Pioneer Press, Sun Current *and other publications. Her short story "Jake" was included in* The Silence of the Loons *anthology. She is Creative Director of Penury Press, a Minnesota publisher of regional mysteries and mirth. She was the editor on* Who Died In Here?, *25 mystery short stories involving crimes that occur in the bathroom. Her first novel,* Stand-up and Die, *is based in Minnesota.*

Pat also works as a humorist entertaining at Fortune 500 events, retirement roasts, women's expos, and civic organizations across the country. Her 1,000-plus performances include What's So Funny About Being Female?, comedy clubs, corporate events, Women's Expos and national television. She has shared the same stage with Phyllis Diller, David Brenner, Fred Willard, Senator Bob Dole and Senator George McGovern. She can be found at **patdennis.com** *on the virtual world of the internet, or in the real world, at Baker's Square.*

Mother's Day

Pat Dennis

Simply put, he would take from her what she had given him—life.

If it could be called a life, that is: forty-nine years old, fired from another minimum-wage job, sleeping on a rollaway in his mother's sewing room, and staring at the ceiling while wondering why he was so unlucky.

"Carl! Dinner's ready!" his mother yelled from downstairs. "Don't make me miss *Wheel of Fortune*."

"As if," he mumbled as he sat up. Every night it was the same: a hotdish at six and *Wheel of Fortune* at six-thirty.

He opened the door and walked into the hallway. Directly across from the sewing room, where he had slept for the last three years, was Billy's room. Inside the room was a double bed, a Lazy-Boy recliner, a 27" color television, and a window that looked out over the creek. He was not allowed to go into the room.

He trudged downstairs to the kitchen and sat in the same chair he had always sat in. His mother sat at the head of the table and he sat on the side. At the rare times when he did look up from his plate, she was not in his direct view. He preferred it that way. And soon, if his luck changed, he would make that view permanent.

"It's tuna noodle," she said, sliding a filled plate in front of him. "I added peas even though you don't like them. I just do not understand why you don't like peas. Everyone likes peas. You always gotta be so different."

He waited to hear the words, "Billy loved peas." According to his mother, Billy loved everything in the world. Billy was a friggin' angel. But at least since the hunting accident six years ago, he was a dead angel.

Or worse, she'd start talking about his father. She'd made his den into some sort of shrine too, just like his brother's bedroom. She'd go on forever about how his father loved peas, although he remembered his father hated them more than he did. His mother, it seemed, fell in love with his father the day he died. Before that she hated his father as much as she hated him.

But this time she didn't bring up Billy or his father. For a change, she was too happy to illuminate his shortcomings. It was only two days before they left for the Mother's Day celebration at Bear Butte Resort and Casino.

"Did I tell you I found a two-for-one coupon for the Mother's Day buffet at the casino?" she asked him while scooping a mound of hotdish onto her plate. "That's one heck of a deal. That buffet is just great. There's a guy in one of those white chef's hats who'll carve you as much prime rib as you want." She paused and sighed deeply before she added, "I suppose you'll want gambling money."

Carl shook his head no. This time he didn't care about gambling. He knew his fortune wouldn't be made at a penny slot. His personal treasure would arrive by the U.S. of A. mail, straight from his mother's life insurance company.

He had saved all he needed for this weekend. He had enough money to pay cash for their rooms, surprise her with gifts while she gambled at the slots, and then boldly pull out a twenty-dollar bill in the buffet line while announcing to everyone within hearing distance, "Let me pay. It's Mother's Day and you know how much I love you, Mom."

Carl almost choked when he thought about speaking to her on Sunday. When he was a kid, he would make a game of guessing how many days he could go without saying a single word to her. At age eleven, he made it to nine days before he was finally forced to speak. And that was only to tell his mother where his brother Billy was.

Billy, her favorite.

He swallowed one more spoonful of the hotdish before he spoke. He wished he didn't have to, but he had no choice. There was no room for error.

"I got a surprise for you," he mumbled. "I made overnight reservations at Bear Butte. We're not just going up for the day. I got you a Jacuzzi suite. It's your Mother's Day present."

His mother stared at him coldly. "You never gave me a present before."

Yes, I did, he wanted to remind her, *thirty-nine years ago.*

He was ten years old when he made a paper-towel holder in woodshop. He carefully sanded and stained it a dark walnut. The wood had been free in class. He spent two weeks collecting and returning pop bottles to buy the roll of paper towel. *"Why would I want something like this?"* she had told him. She kept the paper towels and tossed the holder into the waste can. He had not forgotten the pain he felt. And sitting next to her now, almost four decades later, he knew he would never let her hurt him again.

"Answer my question," she demanded. "Why are you suddenly giving me a Mother's Day present?"

He shrugged his shoulders and mumbled, "I just wanted to, that's all."

"Hmph," she replied and, except for the crunching of under-cooked noodles, they finished their meal in silence.

The uneasy quiet wasn't broken until two days later when they reached Bear Butte Casino and Resort. The resort was an easy two-hour drive from Minneapolis. Its white stucco structure, trimmed in hot pink and lime green neon, stood along the side of the highway. The complex attracted tourists heading south to the Twin Cities or north to Duluth or Canada. The fifty-foot-high video billboards proclaimed twelve hundred slots, ten blackjack tables, and six Texas Hold'em tables. It was one of the most popular casinos in Minnesota. And on Mother's Day, a seat in front of a nickel slot was as scarce as the sounds of a winning jackpot.

"I found one, Mother," Carl yelled across the den of chain-smoking gamblers. His mother had been searching for an open slot machine since their arrival at the casino, twenty minutes earlier.

Carl noticed that the people seated around him looked up at him. He was hoping their reactions would be that of gentle nods and smiles, acknowledging what a good son he was. But instead, they seemed to be more irritated than anything else. Even a public display of adoration between mother and son couldn't compete with the hypnotic lure of flashing screens and potential wealth.

But at least they heard what I said, Carl thought. *They could testify I was a loving son.*

And he would make sure that people would hear everything he said that weekend. He needed as many witnesses as possible.

Although Edna weighed over three hundred pounds, she moved like a raging gazelle toward the machine. As she ran, her cigarette ashes scattered on the red and green floral patterned carpet. Carl pulled out the chair in front of the slot machine and gestured to his mother to sit down. She slid into the chair and Carl tried to push it closer to the machine.

"What the heck are you doing?" she asked. "Leave my chair alone. I can manage it myself."

"Now, Mom, you know I always take care of you. Do you want something to drink? Do you have enough money to gamble? I can give you a few bucks."

Edna glared at him for a moment before she spoke. "Go away. You know I like to gamble alone."

Carl pulled back. If he didn't need the money from her insurance policy, he would have told her to go to hell. But fifty thousand dollars in cash would turn his life around. And there was also her house. It was worth at least two hundred thousand dollars. If Carl played his cards right, he'd be a quarter of a millionaire before the weekend was over.

'Well, sure, Mom, I'll let you be. I gotta' check us in anyway. I got you the king Jacuzzi suite because of your arthritis…"

"I don't have arthritis," Edna interrupted as she lit another cigarette. She slipped a twenty into the machine. She hit the button and yelled "Uff da" as she hit a mini-jackpot of six dollars and fourteen cents.

Carl continued. "I got me the standard room across the hall. That way I'll be close if you need me."

"I won't need you. I told you to go away so I can gamble in peace."

Carl clinched his mouth tight. He took a deep breath before he opened it to speak in the happy and concerned voice he had practiced for weeks. "Now, I don't want you getting depressed like you usually do if you lose all your money. You know I'll give you what you need." He turned, walking away quickly before she could respond.

He also knew that losing money at a casino never depressed his mother. Her favorite T-shirt was embroidered with slot machines, rolling dice, and the words "I'm gambling my kid's inheritance." She had embroidered it herself.

But this weekend, he wanted everyone to think that depression came easily to her.

"The name's Sandstrom," he told the desk clerk. "I have a reservation for a suite and a standard room across the hall. The suite is for my mother. It's her Mother's Day present."

The young clerk looked up and smiled. "That's really sweet. What a nice present."

Carl smiled back, and for the first time noticed her long black hair and deep brown eyes. Normally, he wouldn't have bothered looking at her. She was completely out of his league. By tomorrow morning, however, not only would he be a rich man, but he would also be a man who would need comforting, a man whose mother had committed suicide.

"My mother has arthritis but I'm afraid that's not all. Sometimes she gets so depressed about losing Billy, my brother. And then of course, when we lost my dad.... I just wanted to give her something that would make her happy for at least one day."

"That is so sad!" she told him. Carl noticed that as her eyes became moist, her large breasts moved to the rhythm of her breathing.

"And if you could, please make sure the suite's on the top floor.

My mother appreciates a good view." The hotel was only three stories high but that was high enough.

The clerk finished checking Carl in. He noticed she gave him the AAA discount, even though he wasn't a member. He was always amazed at how every woman in the world, except for his mother, was a sucker for a hard luck story.

He smiled all the way to the elevators and started to hum "California Dreamin'" as he pressed the third-floor button. Life was good.

Their rooms were at the end of the hallway. That was another reason to smile. It was proof that his luck was changing. He pulled out the card key to his mother's room. The clerk had automatically given him two key cards for each room. He put one of the key cards in his wallet and with the other opened her door.

Rose-colored walls and a quilt-covered king-sized bed made the room inviting. In the corner sat a large whirlpool surrounded by glistening glass blocks. But Carl was interested only in the windows. In the advertisements they were noted to be not only large but could also be partially opened to allow access to the fresh northern air and the scent of pine trees, and, if he unscrewed just enough hinges, to the concrete below.

He looked at the alarm clock on the side table. It was 3:45. In a half hour, he would surprise his mother, again. But first, he had work to do.

He removed the vinyl gloves he had packed in his overnight bag and put them on. He took out a screwdriver and a coarse file. He carefully unscrewed the hinges, removing the screws. He carried the screws to the bathroom and lifted the toilet seat. There he stood, filing the small screws, letting the metal shavings fall into the water.

He was proud of himself for being so careful. But there was a lot at stake. It was not only the money he so desperately wanted. He wanted a chance, for once in his life, to do something right, even if it was wrong.

When he was through, he flushed the toilet and went back to the windows. He replaced the screws and jiggled the frame.

His mother was just as tall as he, but weighed at least 100 pounds more. In the middle of the night he would enter her room. He would not turn on the light but would wake her and tell her the hotel was on fire. In the dark, he would grab her hand, guide her off the side of the bed, and lead her to the window. He knew she would still be half-drunk. He would tell her the hallway was on fire and to lean out of the window and breathe in the air. And with one quick push she would easily crash through the loosened window frame to her death.

He had only one more chore to accomplish before he left the room to search out his mother. From a zippered pouch on the side of his bag he removed a small note wrapped in Saran Wrap. He removed the note that rested inside. For months he had been learning to forge his mother's handwriting. The short note, written on her own notepaper that was surely covered in her fingerprints, was perfect.

"*I'm too depressed to go on*," it read.

That was it. Six words that would change Carl's life forever.

He pulled open the drawer and slipped the note inside the one place he was certain his mother would not look: The Gideon Bible.

He smiled and nodded his head once more in satisfaction as he looked around the room. He left the suite, dropped his bag off in his room across the hall, and went down to the casino floor.

"Surprise!" Carl yelled as he walked down the Pennies from Heaven slot aisle. He was carrying a dozen yellow roses. The yellow roses had been hidden in his van, underneath his Green Bay Packer's jacket. He knew his mother would never pick up the jacket. Carl was the only Packer fan in the entire Sandstrom family.

This time, everyone in the aisle turned to look at him. A few even smiled. When he finally reached his mother he tried to hand her the roses.

"How the heck am I going to gamble and hold flowers at the same time? Carl, I swear, sometimes you don't have the brains of an animal cracker."

Carl stood there holding the flowers, humiliated.

"Put them in the hotel room. You got any more surprises up your sleeve? Balloons? Maybe a friggin' parade?"

He assumed his mother was on a losing streak. Because, if it were possible, she was even nastier than normal when she was losing.

But that was a bonus for him. If the police did investigate the death of a depressed woman who had lost both a son and a husband, knowledge of her gambling losses would help to determine it was suicide.

Carl reached into his back pocket and pulled out a king size Pearson Nut Roll candy bar, his mother's favorite.

"This was going to be your next surprise," he told her and then thought, *at least for now, until you splatter on the parking lot.*

"Hmmph," she mumbled and took the bar, sliding it into her purse.

"I'll meet you in front of the buffet at six and don't forget I'm buying."

"Buying what? Your own meal? I'm the one with the two-for-one coupon."

Carl stomped off, repeating over and over to himself that in only a few more hours he would not only be free, he would also be rich.

He spent the rest of the afternoon in his hotel room watching television. He was going to order movies off the porn channel but decided against it. He didn't want the young hotel to clerk to think he was a pervert. He didn't want to blow his chance with her like he'd blown so many other chances in life.

At ten to six he headed downstairs to the buffet.

"Happy Mother's Day again," Carl said to his mother who was already waiting in line and stamping her foot in anger. She stared at the wristwatch on her arm.

"You were almost late," she spat out.

Good, Carl thought, good. She's gotta' be losing a lot of money.

"Now, now Mother." He smiled at the people around him, giving them a sort of see what I have to put up with but I love her anyway look.

Edna pulled out her coupon. Her dinner was the free one and Carl paid for his.

The buffet was excellent. Edna went back four times for prime rib and twice for ham. She filled her plate with tiny egg rolls, crispy wontons and mashed potatoes with gravy. She loaded up on Indian fry bread and had three desserts. She became angry when she couldn't find any artificial sweetener for her usual after dinner coffee.

"Don't they know people watch their diet?" she asked, as her eyes searched the room for their waitress. "I give up. Don't you dare tip her! I'm going to go gamble."

Carl pulled out his wallet and removed a fifty-dollar bill and held it up high in air before he said, "Here Mom, I know you're losing so this should help you out."

Once again, he saw that people around him took notice of his generosity.

Edna quickly grabbed the fifty and put it inside her bra.

"Whattya' mean losing? I'm up seven hundred dollars."

Edna shuffled off in haste.

Carl just sat there. The news of her winning wasn't good. But there was still a chance she'd lose it all before the night was over. He'd seen it happen to her before. And soon she'd start having her usual after-dinner cocktail or two, or seven. She'd be sloshed before she hit the sack.

He just had to learn patience. The hours would pass soon enough.

Carl had a few dollars left and decided to go back to the casino. He decided it would be wise to gamble near his mother so he could point out the "dear sweet woman" to others. The dearness and sweetness of her would be easier to pitch if the other people weren't anywhere near her.

He slid into a nickel Enchanted Forest slot. He loved that machine. If three eyes popped upon the screen at the same time, every line would be a winner. Carl played the minimum, nine lines at a nickel each for a total of 45 cents. Within a half-hour he was completely broke.

He could use the fifty bucks his mother took from him but

he wasn't about to ask her for anything. He sat for a few minutes before someone asked him if he was playing "his machine." The casino was too crowded for Carl to sit at a machine without playing it. And, the only place to sit was in front of a machine or a table. He decided that he had watched his mother long enough and he would go back to his room and wait.

In his room, Carl watched five hours of the Shopping Network. He picked up the phone twice to call but changed his mind each time. Since he didn't have a credit card he wanted to know if they would accept a C.O.D. He hung up when he realized it might take more than a few days for the check to arrive.

The second time he desperately wanted to order the "stainless steel men's chronograph watch complete with both calendar and luminous silver-tone hour and minute hands created from diamond chips." The cost was only nine hundred and ninety nine dollars and forty-five cents. It was guaranteed to be forty-one percent off the retail price.

He continued watching until 11:10 p.m. when he heard his mother enter her suite across the hall. He turned off the television and sat in the dark, watching the alarm clock slowly change its display. At 11:40 he opened his door and walked across the hall.

He gently inserted the key card into the slot and opened the door. He knew her habits. She would have smoked one cigarette before she changed into her nightgown. She would then remove her make-up and brush her teeth. Finally, she would slather night cream all over her face. She would relent and have one more cigarette before she fell asleep so soundly that she wouldn't hear a fire siren or a child's cry.

The room was dark when he opened the door. He crept in, past the bathroom, down the hall, and glanced at the blankets mounded high over her body.

He walked quietly to the window and cranked it open slowly. He turned around, ready to yell "Mom! Fire! Get to the window!" when his mother bounded across the room from where she had been hiding in the corner. Her enormous body lunged at him and with one quick shove, sent him skyrocketing out the window.

Carl smiled one more time before he died. It wasn't his life that passed in front of him as he fell but his father's and brother's deaths. He saw his mother yanking the ladder out from under his father as he climbed off the roof. He saw his mother holding the rifle over Billy's lifeless body. Carl briefly wondered if she would turn the sewing room into a shrine for him as she did for Billy.

And he smiled knowing that for a little while, he would be her favorite.

Carl Brookins

Before he became a mystery writer and reviewer, Brookins was a freelance photographer, a Public Television program director and producer, a Cable TV administrator, and a counselor and faculty member at Metropolitan State University in St. Paul, Minnesota. He has reviewed mystery fiction for the St. Paul Pioneer Press *and for* Mystery Scene Magazine. *His reviews also appear on his own web site, and on Internet review sites, including Books n' Bytes and The Mystery Morgue. Brookins is an avid recreational sailor. With his wife and friends he has sailed in many locations across the world. He is a member of Mystery Writers of America, Sisters in Crime, and Private Eye Writers of America. He can frequently be found touring bookstores and libraries with his companions-in-crime-fiction, The Minnesota Crime Wave.*

He writes a sailing adventure series featuring Michael Tanner and Mary Whitney, the latest titled Old Silver, *and the Sean Sean private investigator detective series.* The Case of the Greedy Lawyers *is currently available. Writing as Avery Ames, his first academic novel,* Bloody Halls, *will be released late in 2007. He is married with two grown daughters and lives with his wife Jean, a retired publisher and editor, in Roseville, Minnesota.*

A Fish Story

Carl Brookins

W hat do you think?"

"About what? That ridiculous looking outfit you have on?" Catherine squinted at me through the early-morning gloom. It was, after all, only five-fifteen on a summer morning UP NORTH. That's where we were, UP NORTH in this small but substantial log cabin perched on a rocky promontory jutting out from the shore of some lake in Northern Minnesota. Burnt something, I think it was named. How appropriate, considering the constant sun. Third day of this so-called vacation.

"I read about wood ticks and deer ticks and avian whatever and West Nile scourge, so I figured I should be protected. Don't you want me to be protected?"

Catherine smothered what I took to be a grin. I had to admit, privately, she looked fetching in her short shorts and blue tennies. She wiped a tiny line of sweat from her forehead. This early and she was already sweating. Great. Or maybe it was the strain of trying not to let her grin turn into an out-loud laugh.

I didn't care. Look. I'm a small guy and so I think I'm more vulnerable to all these esoteric and exotic maladies that doctors are always talking about on TV and in the newspapers. Personally I didn't see why anyone would even want to go UP NORTH to a resort or a camp of some kind. This was a vacation? Northern Minnesota is chock full of resorts. Why this one?

Vacation to me meant kicking back in some place with people around to bring drinks and maybe massage your feet and serve up a few great meals. If there had to be water around it would be contained in a nice warm well-treated swimming pool. Maybe with a hot tub on the side. One with soothing jets. Not this place with tall pines, log cabins and rocks and a thin sand beach. Oh yeah, and boats. The narrow kind. A tippy canoe. Just what I wanted to ride around in. Yes, I can swim, of course I can, but swimming in the frigid waters of this lake was not my idea of relaxation.

"Sean," Catherine said, still trying, I believed, to keep the laughter out of her voice. The fact that she was taller than I and a lot better looking didn't help. "Sean, you'll die in the sun in that getup. Lose the long-sleeved shirt. Besides, those loud checks just aren't you. What you need is a light shirt, a liberal spritzing with some Deet. A cap, shorts and don't forget the sunscreen."

Somebody banged on the door. "C'mon, Sean Sean. The sun is up and we've got to get out on the lake. All the best fishing spots will be taken." I detected the familiar voice of my friend, ace Ramsey County prosecutor Jerry Ford. He was an inexhaustible and inveterate outdoors type, in spite of the gimp he'd sustained as a result of a gunshot to the knee. He and his wife, Paige, were in the other half of this cabin, called Thor's Parlor, or something ridiculous like that.

I yanked open the door. That door required a hefty yank because it didn't fit all that well in the frame. Something about wood and humidity. With the door open and Jerry Ford's grinning face in front of me, I could hear a bunch of noisy urchins in the distance. I stepped out and looked across the campground to see a large crowd of children, mostly pre-teens with their camp counselors, gathering in front of the big lodge that served as a kind of unofficial office at street—er, ground—level. The camp spread out among some very tall pine trees along the lake shore.

Catherine had been after me for years to reserve a week at this place. As an inducement she told me about the log sauna right at the edge of the lake. It seemed one could journey north to the edge of the Boundary Waters Canoe Area in mid-winter, shelter in an uninsulated cabin, chop wood or provide some other maintenance, and sauna of an evening. Great, but then what? Oh, Catherine said, somebody chops a hole in the lake ice at the end of the short ramp and you jump out of the sauna and into the freezing lake!

Sound like fun? Forget it! Anyway, this was summer and a sauna didn't appeal right now.

I had finally succumbed to Catherine's and Ford's blandishments and agreed to this week in the woods. Adding insult, today Ford insisted he and I make like woodsmen and go fish for our supper. Hunters and gatherers we would be. At least we wouldn't be hunting big game. To me, charging around the woodlands with a high-powered rifle trying to pot Bambi or one of his relatives didn't seem like much of a sport. But, maybe that's because when I hunt with a weapon, the critters I go after in the canyons and hills of the city have two legs and like as not shoot back.

Y'see, I'm a short, red-Ked-wearing private investigator. An urban private shamus. And in spite of what some critics will tell you about the real life of a private detective, I do sometimes come up against bad guys with guns.

★ ★ ★

Ford and I had been sitting in the aforementioned canoe for several hours. It was hot on the water. There was almost no breeze and the sweat trickling out of my armpits was not a pleasant by-product. Ford, in the stern, was casting. He'd been doing that nearly the whole time. Me, I tried casting about five times and snarled up the line three of those times. Now I opted for hanging the line over the side of the canoe hoping nothing else would bite on the spinner that was attached to something called a leader that was, in turn, attached to a long spool of fishing line—some sort of monofilament—all neatly wrapped around a contraption called a reel at the end of a flexible tube labeled a rod.

We'd caught two fish. Ford called 'em "nice-sized walleyes." To be precise, I'd caught them. Ford, the perpetual casting machine, hadn't even had a strike. So we'd caught some fish, drunk some beer, eaten some sandwiches and paddled around the lake's northeast edge from fishing spot to fishing spot. Now we were about a quarter-mile east from where we'd started, and my feet, in my white-soled red Keds, were hot and getting itchy.

Ford grunted something and I looked up. I guess my eyes had sort of closed. "What?"

"I said, look at that." He was staring at the shore, only a few yards away. He pointed with his paddle. He'd directed me to stop paddling when we reached the swampy edge of a little bay where there were several old dead trees, some lying in the water, a nasty tangle of dead wood just waiting beneath the surface to snag the unwary nimrod. I looked where he pointed. I could make out what appeared to be a torn piece of cloth snagged on a dead branch. The piece of cloth wasn't faded from sun and rain so it hadn't been there very long. It was bright blue and looked to my eagle eye like a piece of a blouse or shirt.

"Let's get a little closer."

"Watch it," Jerry said in a quiet tone. "We could get hung up on these dead-heads."

It took several minutes of maneuvering the canoe until we got close enough so I could pluck the scrap off the sharp branch. The pointed end of the branch was bright, unlike the brownish-gray weathered length. I rested the paddle on my knees and examined the scrap of cloth. There was a smear of something dark on the single torn edge. The other edges were nicely hemmed. I sniffed it. Smelled like blood. Not very old blood. Maybe a little sweat and something else. I told Jerry. He frowned and glanced around.

"Must be from some camper who was here last week."

"I don't think so, Jerry. This hasn't been rained on. And we've got what looks like blood. I'd say this cloth hasn't been here much over four or five hours."

He frowned some more and we backed out of the tangle. Fishing disappeared from my mind. We got clear of the submerged tangle of weeds and downed trees and turned around. I put the scrap into a plastic baggie and dropped it beside the tackle box. Two strong strokes on the paddle and we started back to camp. At that moment the brake on my rod chattered. Fortunately my reflexes were still good and I grabbed the rod Jerry had loaned me—I don't own any fishing gear—and held it up so the snag wouldn't pull the rod over the side of the boat. I twiddled with the reel and line began to scream out into the lake.

"Keep the tip up!" Jerry hollered.

Suddenly the line stopped running out.

"Reel 'im in," Ford counseled. So I cranked, keeping as much tension on the line as I could. For several minutes I fought the fish as it made runs away, back toward the canoe, out toward the open lake. Always I kept pulling the damn thing closer. Sweat poured off me, staining my shirt. Flies buzzed around my head and my hat fell off. I could feel my brain beginning to cook as I fought the fish and the fish fought back.

Finally the line was pointing almost straight down, the rod was sharply curved, and the fish seemed to be resting. Suddenly with no warning, the line slackened, the rod tip snapped upright and the fish rose thrashing right to the surface. Madly I wound. What I saw then at the water's surface, was a huge maw of sharp white teeth at one end of a long dark body. The head whipped right and left, snapped the metal leader clean off the swivel. With another splash it disappeared as suddenly as it had risen out of the dark water.

"Holy moley," Jerry said in an awed voice. "That thing was huge. Must have gone fifteen, maybe twenty pounds!"

★ ★ ★

"I lost a big fish," I greeted Catherine when we arrived back at the cabin. She looked worried.

"I'll say! It was huge! Where's Paige?" crowed Jerry.

"I don't know. Something strange has happened. I think we've been robbed and I can't find Paige. I'm getting worried. She's been gone a long time."

Ford turned and bolted around the cabin, heading for his own section. I ran after him and clutched his arm just as he burst through the screen.

"Hold it! Hold it! Let's go cautiously here." He dragged me a step or two and then stopped. I held on to his arm and sidestepped so I could see into the cabin. This side was a duplicate of ours, except reversed. One large room with a kitchen area, a small table, a couple of beat-up chairs and a double bed in one corner. Most of the walls, except for the corner partitioned off for the bathroom, had sliding windows with screens. Just like our side. Catherine had not followed us.

"What do you see, Jerry?" I said. He nodded, calmed down a little.

We both jammed our hands into our back pants pockets and stared first at the floor which showed no tracks, just some scattered granules of sand. I bent over, easier for me with my short legs, and peered at the sand. It looked a lot like beach sand, but it appeared to have been spilled, rather than tracked in on somebody's shoes.

I could hear Jerry's breathing, short, hard gasps. "Look at this," he said.

I looked. Sure enough there was a smear of damp dark fluid and a couple of dark hairs on the edge of the table. The hair looked like Paige's and the fluid looked like blood. It was drying around the edges.

"My wallet's gone," said Jerry, peering at the table by the bed. "So's Paige's purse. Our camera."

"Much money?"

"I think we were carrying a couple of hundred between us."

"We better call the sheriff," I said.

"What? Oh, yes. Catherine!" Jerry raised his voice and Catherine appeared at the door behind us. "I think we better call in the law," Jerry said in a low tremulous voice.

"I'll go to the lodge and do it. Our cells don't work up here because of the iron ore in the ground." Catherine turned and walked out of sight.

"Oh, God," Jerry whispered. He leaned against the wall and then slid down until he was sitting on the plank floor. He leaned his head forward against his knees, closing his eyes.

"Kids in camp, you think?"

Ford shook his head. "I can't believe it. Not this camp. I don't know. My God, Sean, Paige might be seriously hurt."

"Stay here," I said. I took a long breath and went outside, staring closely at the sandy ground around the cabin. There were plenty of tracks. I found a trail of familiar looking footprints leading away from Ford's door to our side of the cabin. Whoever made them didn't seem to be in a hurry, judging from the stride length. Walking, not running. The tracks led in a meander down to the beach and into the water as if the person had gotten into a boat or maybe a canoe. I could see other tracks where Ford and I had come ashore after our fishing trip. That reminded me.

I returned to the cabin. Ford hadn't moved from his place by the wall. I touched the blood smear on the edge of the table and rubbed a bit between my fingers. I smelled it. It was blood all right. Then I went to our side of Thor's Parlor and looked at the scrap of cloth we'd retrieved that morning.

It looked like the piece might be from the tail of a woman's blouse. It also looked and smelled familiar. I detected that same odor when I was in the other part of the cabin. A faint odor of a woman's cologne. It was Paige's favorite, but I couldn't recall ever seeing the blouse.

Catherine reappeared and said, "They'll send a deputy but it will be a little while."

"Okay. Why don't you go next door and see to Jerry. He looked to be in a bad way."

She turned and left, touching me lightly on the arm. I went back to the beach and after walking along the shore for a little way, peering down at the sand, found a place where someone might have come ashore recently. The rock was still damp and close by I found a single track in the soft ground. I needed Natty Bumpo to track this sign. He wasn't available, so I was left with my own meager tracking skills. For a hot sweaty hour in sun and shade, brambles and thickets, I walked around the resort mostly bent over with my nose to the ground, following a trail that began to look like whoever had made it was drunk or deliberately making tracks for the fun of it. What would Lew Archer do in this situation? I figured he'd sit down and think about it, consider the ramifications of those who might be involved and draw a conclusion or two that could lead to a course of action. So I did that.

I found a rock with a sunny side and a shady side and no mosquitoes worthy of comment. I was far enough from the camp that I couldn't even hear the rug rats at the beach. I sat down by my big boulder and thought about what I knew and what I could conjecture from the facts. What came to me was the beginning of a suspicion that Paige was not in imminent danger. Her tracks, if they were hers, didn't give me a message of panic, or even running. In fact, I was beginning to think she might even be directly involved in the theft of the money, wallets and digital camera Jerry had told me were missing. An hour, more or less, passed peacefully. I heard nary a single siren. Truth to tell, I dozed. When I wasn't dozing I thought some more about the scrap of cloth, the blood, the hairs, the sand on the cabin floor and the tracks. Tracks that finally disappeared in the clearing near the gravel road. Did the thief flee in a vehicle? He, or she, must have driven off. Surely she, or he, or they, weren't tromping through the underbrush of the BWCA or paddling madly to the other side of the lake. I made a mental note to ask about missing vehicles, including canoes. Motor boat? I hadn't heard a single one since we returned to camp.

Insects buzzed about and the temperature rose a little. There was only the slightest breeze. An unseen critter rustled through the grass and twigs nearby. When I awoke from my second doze, I was pretty sure I knew what had happened and how. "Why" was still out to lunch, although I had an idea about that. I had to check one more thing. So I went back to our cabin.

Neither Catherine nor Ford was there, but I could hear people talking off in the direction of the big lodge. My hot feet itched in my red Keds so I changed into the other pair I had brought. They were right where I had left them when I unpacked two days earlier, and they were cool because they were a little damp.

I sauntered out to the big lodge where I found Catherine, Ford and several parents in camp. The director, a pleasant older fellow, was also there. Goody, an audience. Most everybody turned to watch me approach.

When I drew closer I spoke up. "Most of you know that in my professional life, I'm a private investigator. And, modestly, I'll tell you that I'm pretty good at it. But this case has me in a quandary."

There were murmurs.

"Oh, you weren't aware that we've had a theft? Yes, and perhaps even some serious injury to one of the guests. However," I held up a hand to quell the rising sounds of concern from my audience. "However, I believe I can set your minds at rest. I do admit to being stumped for the moment. That is, I don't know where the boodle has got to, although I have my suspicions. More on that in a moment.

"Let me just go through the events so you will see how my reasoning worked. There were three, possibly four perpetrators of this caper. Three I have identified. This was a carefully planned theft, organized by a cunning and clever mind, abetted by at least two individuals who should know better.

"This caper began about five this morning. At least two of the gang sneaked away from camp undetected in order to plant some evidence." Here I reached into the brown grocery bag I had placed at my feet and held up for all to see the scrap of cloth Ford and I had retrieved while fishing. Out of the corner of my eye I saw Jerry Ford turning his face away.

"If you examine this scrap carefully, you'll see that while it was torn from the tail of a woman's blouse, in order to start the tear, the hem was cut, indicating, possibly, a deliberate act, rather than a tear made during hasty flight. Now you may wonder how the scrap of cloth got to the tree where Ford and I found it later in the morning. I'm fairly certain two female conspirators paddled out early in the morning to plant the scrap. I recall that while it was quite cool this morning and I had only finished dressing, my friend was dressed and perspiring lightly, as if she'd been out chopping wood, or perhaps paddling a canoe."

"Pretty thin, I say," remarked Catherine, looking me right in the eye.

A good actor, Catherine.

I smiled. "Then there's the matter of the blood smear on the table in Ford's cabin. Even though it's not a good idea to tamper with possible evidence, I touched the blood and smelled it and am certain it is not of human origin. I have no doubt Paige sacrificed a little hair from her scalp, or perhaps from her brush which seemed remarkably free of hair when I recently examined it, but she drew the line at giving a few drops of blood to the cause."

I turned toward him. "Ford, you are a pretty good actor, but I'm amazed you didn't rush out immediately to call in the law, which you would have in a real case of robbery, injury and abduction. That's right. This is not a real case and I'll tell you why I know that. Catherine was able to deflect the possible entanglement with the local law by volunteering to call the police—how long ago, my dear? I noticed that even after quite some time there is no siren to be heard behind the cries of happy children and the twittering of critters. Now, I'm somewhat unfamiliar with the way such things work in this rural area. But it seems to me that after about two hours I should have heard a siren and we should have a deputy sheriff in our laps. A siren, that is, if you'd injected enough anxiety into the message. I'm betting you never made that call.

"Then I took a look at that spread of sand on the floor of the cabin. It just didn't look tracked in. In fact, I think it might have been thrown there by hand. Well, those things put me on my guard. I looked more closely at the tracks and began to follow them about the place. Reexamined the evidence, you might say. That's something good detectives do quite often.

"The tracks wandered about a good bit and they didn't seem to be the spoor of someone in distress or of a thief trying to make tracks away from the scene of a crime. They had more the appearance of someone taking a casual stroll around the camp, laying a false trail, as it were. By then I had my guard up and I thought those tracks I followed looked familiar. I knew I had not been in those places even though I was wearing shoes that left those identical tracks. So I sauntered back to the cabin to check my other pair of shoes, and what did I find? You may well ask."

I reached into the brown paper bag and held up a pair of red tennis shoes, identical to those I was wearing. "Here was a pair of almost new tennis shoes I had not yet worn this week. They should have been clean and even pristine. But what I saw was a damp and sandy residue on the bottoms. That clinched it. I said to myself this is no robbery, there is no injury here, this is a prank, a conspiracy by at least three people who should know better than to have a little fun with this investigator.

"I now formally accuse my good friend Jerry Ford, not a half-bad actor, my good friend Catherine, an excellent actor, and Jerry's wife Paige, standing back there in the bushes trying unsuccessfully to remain hidden while nearly doubled over with laughter."

I pointed and bowed in her direction. "I heard your car drive up," I smirked. "The one with that peculiar and distinctive whine when it shuts off."

Paige laughed aloud and held up their "missing" digital camera. She flashed a picture while the six other people arrayed around us applauded politely.

"What was this all about?" I asked. "You thought I was bored, up here in the weeds and woods? Nothing to engage my keen mind other than some scammy puzzle? Oh, wait, I've got it! YOU guys got a little bored! Hah!"

"Okay, okay," chuckled Jerry, leaning on a broadly smiling Catherine, "you got us. Now tell us about the big fish you almost caught this morning. You know, the one that got away?"

Joel Arnold

Joel Arnold lives in Savage, Minnesota, with his wife, two kids and collection of old typewriters. His writing has appeared in over three-dozen publications, ranging from Cat Fancy *to* Weird Tales. *"Leave No Wake" is his first foray into the mystery genre, and he's currently working on a novel-length mystery involving National Park employees. He has many fond memories of Minnesota resorts, including the smell of the family dog rolling on rotting fish carcasses, and accidentally setting a hook in his brother's eyelid while casting for perch. He'd love to hear from you at **joelarnold@mchsi.com.***

Leave No Wake

Joel Arnold

I leaned against the gas pump stationed at the end of the dock and sipped from a lukewarm bottle of orange juice. Benny Helstrom's hail-pocked aluminum canoe pulled silently up. "How're they hitting today?" I asked, nodding at the half-dozen turtles crawling over each other on the floor of his canoe.

He tossed a loop of rope around one of the pilings and shook his head. "Sons of bitches are scarce as shit today, Mr. Varney. Scarce as shit."

I realized long ago that there was nothing stopping the vulgarities that tumbled from the eleven-year-old's mouth, so I'd long since given up. His mother worked two jobs, and his father had run out on them when he was only five. Besides, the kid was good at heart. If I've learned anything from my seventy-two years, it is the importance of keeping things in perspective.

"What'll it be this morning?" I asked.

"The usual." Benny held out two crisp dollar bills. The town of Nisswa paid him a buck per turtle for the weekly turtle races, and at the end of each race day, Benny gathered them up and released them back into the wild.

I waved the bills away. "Keep 'em." I walked over the aluminum dock planks and up cement steps sunk into a small rise of land. On top was Arrow Point Resort's lodge, a brown wooden building that served as shop, front desk, and owners' quarters, the owners being me and Noah Johnson. We had eight cabins for rent, plus space for some RVs and tents. Aside from the playground, shuffleboard, and a small beach with diving raft, we offered the most beautiful sunsets this side of the Mississippi.

The screen door slapped shut behind me, and I noticed that the cash register drawer stuck out like a squared-off tongue. "Noah!" I called to the back room. "Drawer's open. Again." I heard nothing in reply, but there looked to be no cash missing, the thin piles of bills arranged tidily in their appropriate slots.

Not only was Noah my business partner of thirty years, he was also selectively hard of hearing. He'd turned eighty the previous month, and if I recall correctly, he'd turned eighty the previous year, as well. For the most part, the older residents of Nisswa thought of us as a couple of old bachelors, but I think deep down they had us figured out, and that was fine with me.

Besides, we had the only boat-gas pump for miles around; boaters pulled up to the dock, filled their tanks, then walked up to the shop to pay. More often than not, they bought a soda, beer, ice cream, maybe even night crawlers or a bucket of minnows. There's a whole mess of lakes up here, connected to each other by calm, quiet channels: Nisswa, Roy, Spider, Bass and Upper Gull Lakes, and of course, the enormous Gull Lake. We were on an isthmus dividing Bass from Upper Gull, and our dock jutted out into a section of narrows edged with water lilies. Boats passed slowly by whether or not they stopped for gas, heeding the Leave No Wake signs on either end of the channel.

I shut the cash drawer with a sigh, reached into the glass display case for a pack of bubble gum, and retrieved a cold Mountain Dew from the fridge. Back at the dock, I handed them to Benny and helped push his canoe off into the still, morning water.

"Thanks, Mr. Varney. I'm tired as shit today."

I nodded and waved as the foul-mouthed turtle boy disappeared amidst the water lilies and the glare of the rising sun. The smell of wet turtle lingered in my nostrils, so I inhaled deeply, filling my lungs with the scent of lake, pine, and gasoline, bracing myself for the day.

★ ★ ★

The McMahon family from Duluth checked in just before noon, over two hours early.

"We don't have the beds made up, yet," Noah, fresh from a nap, informed Mr. McMahon, while his wife and two teenaged sons waited in the car.

McMahon grinned. "Don't bother. We bring our own linens."

Noah looked confused. "We do wash our sheets every day."

"It's my wife," McMahon said. "What can I do? She's seen Oprah a few too many times—worried about germs."

"We only got good germs around here," Noah insisted.

"No offense. It's just the wife…"

My back was to Noah while I restocked the cigarettes, and I turned just in time to see Mrs. McMahon get out of the car carrying a bucketful of Pine-Sol, Lysol, Tilex—you name it. She set the bucket on the hood of the car and searched through it until she found a bottle of mosquito repellent, which she sprayed over her body.

McMahon noticed me looking, and shrugged. He arched his eyebrows as if to say, "Told you so."

A pair of fishermen checked in next, dressed in waders, camouflaged fishing vests and caps with slogans of beer companies stitched above the brims. Jim Blanchard and Chuck Regal. Jim was the smaller of the two, with huge, brown muttonchops peppered with stray crumbs.

"How's the fishing?" he asked.

Noah ran Blanchard's credit card through the machine. "The northerns are nibbling, the bass are biting, the perch are prodding, but the walleyes, by all accounts and estimations, are withholding."

I stepped up next to Noah, kicking him lightly behind the counter. "The fishing's fine," I reassured the two men. "The fishing's just fine."

Michael and Lynette Perry, twenty-something newlyweds, arrived next. The groom had called ahead and ordered champagne and a box of truffles from the Chocolate Ox to be waiting on their bed. The wedding occurred two days previous, and the glow on their faces and new gold rings had yet to wear off. The back window of their SUV still held traces of soaped letters.

"Sunset should be a nice one tonight," Noah said. "Should peak around eight-oh-seven."

The Perrys smiled indulgently at Noah and took their key.

★ ★ ★

Late afternoon, I shook out a small handful of pills from a plastic container divided into the days of the week and handed them to Noah. The container was supposed to help him remember to take his pills each day, but I'd become part of the dispensing equation years ago when it became apparent that Noah rarely remembered what day it was. He swallowed the pills two at a time, chasing them with swigs of iced tea. He cocked his head and nodded towards the door. "Someone's coming," he said.

The screen door opened and closed, and the scent of perfume, cigarettes and beer preceded the lone woman who entered.

Her name was Gina Veale, and we learned later that she came from one of the strip clubs out on Highway 10. But that afternoon, she hoisted a brown leather purse onto the counter and dug through it, pulling out a wad of crumpled tens and twenties. "I'd just like to stay a few nights."

Noah wrinkled his nose at the condition of the bills and carefully straightened them out, facing them the same way and placing them neatly into the register. I slid a registration card over the top of the counter, and after she filled it out, I handed her the key to cabin ten.

She tapped an unlit cigarette on the counter and looked out the screen door at the narrow one-way dirt road that led here.

"You all right?" I asked.

She looked at me for a moment. "I used to come up here when I was a little girl," she said. "Before my daddy died." She smiled, and it seemed like a hard won smile. "In fact, I remember you," she said.

I looked at her closely, trying to remember, trying to reconcile her face with any of the thousands of children who had stayed here over the years, but I couldn't place her. She had a narrow nose and dimpled chin, dishwater blonde hair and a yellow tank top that revealed the tattoo of a broken heart between her shoulder blades. On the small of her back was a series of Chinese characters.

Noah had a faded SEMPER FI on his left bicep, but his do-or-die days now consisted of tending the lodge and rocking on the porch, scanning the Nisswa *Dispatch* obits to reassure himself he was still alive.

"Sorry to hear about your father," I said. "Mine's gone, too."

Ms. Veale squinted at me, and I figured it had been a stupid thing to say since at my age, of course my father was gone. I coughed lightly into my fist. "I'm glad you decided to give us another try. If you need anything, let us know."

★ ★ ★

Aside from our renters, there was a slow but steady stream of customers needing gas for their thirsty boats. The fishermen, Regal and Blanchard, came in to buy a case of Bud, and a short time later they left in a red pickup, probably to hit the bars in Brainerd or the casino in Hinckley. The McMahon teenagers bought ice cream sandwiches and Cokes and rented a paddleboat. Both were clean-cut and skinny, the older of the two sullen, the younger one wearing a perpetual smirk. The father had been in the shop earlier asking about local golf courses, and the mother—I figured she was holed up in their cabin cleaning, scouring and disinfecting the germ-infected rooms. I chuckled.

Noah spent most of the afternoon napping in the living room behind the shop. His relationship with his afternoon naps was much more torrid than anything he and I shared together. And when he wasn't napping, he often sat on his recliner listening to old vinyl records of Count Basie and Duke Ellington. They popped and hissed, but the sound was warm, like the saturated hues of an old Technicolor movie.

The way his mind had deteriorated in the last few years, I sometimes wondered how much time we had left together, how much quality time. But no matter what, I'd be there for him, like I knew he'd be there for me if things had been turned around.

I needed some fresh air.

I raked the small patch of beach and swept the docks, circling the property, picking up stray pieces of litter as I went. Some might call it puttering, but I'd never admit to it. I checked the fish-cleaning house, making sure the counters were spic and span, then checked the small hut where we kept our live minnows in a bath of running water.

111

Everything was good, including the weather, and I saw Gina Veale sitting on a wicker chair on the redwood deck of her cabin, looking out across Bass Lake, a cigarette in one hand, a beer in the other. She looked hungry and lost and sad.

"Is there anything I can get you?" I offered, standing on the slope of shore next to the deck.

She slowly looked over at me and shook her head. "No," she said. "Thanks. Everything's just fine." Then she pointed to the lily pads that stretched out from the shore. "When I was here as a little girl, I caught a couple of turtles out there. I put them in my daddy's minnow bucket. Gave them names. Timmy and Tommy. Funny I remember that. Timmy and Tommy Turtle. But then I had to let them go before we left." She smiled thinly. "I cried," she said. "I really wanted to bring them home."

I nodded and smiled, not knowing what to say. But she waved a ring of smoke from her face and said, "Maybe they're still out there. Do you think so?" She took a sip of beer. "Timmy and Tommy."

She watched me expectantly, as if she really wanted me to remember her, and I tried, I really did, but how many kids had I seen here? How many little girls? And to transpose one of those small hopeful faces onto this adult? It just wasn't possible.

"You have a good night," I said, and walked quietly away so as to let her be with her memories.

★ ★ ★

The trouble started shortly before the sun readied itself to set on Upper Gull. A family of loons warbled close to shore, turtles poked their heads up between the water lilies, and bullfrogs started warming up for their nightly keening.

A black SUV set high over fat wheels slid to a stop on the gravel driveway in front of our shop, and a man in a tank top and Bermuda shorts got out, sunglasses hiding his eyes, short-cropped hair sticking up through a layer of sweat and gel. He stopped short of our door when he spotted Gina smoking outside her cabin. He turned toward her.

"Hey!" he called.

Gina tossed her cigarette when she saw him and turned toward her cabin's door, knocking over an empty beer can.

"Gina, wait, damn it!"

"Stay away from me," she said.

"Wait! Gina!"

"Fuck off." For some reason, she couldn't get her door open.

He jogged toward her. "What do you think you're doing? You think you can just run away? You didn't think I'd find out where you went?"

"Leave me alone." She got the door open and slid in, but when she tried to shut the cabin door, he wedged his foot against the jamb and reached inside, yanking her out by her upper arm.

I figured it was time to get involved. "Let go of her!" I shouted.

The man pulled her toward his truck and I stomped toward them, waving my hand in the air. "Stop that right now. What do you think you're doing?"

He ignored me as he opened the passenger door and shoved Gina roughly inside. He slapped her across the face. I grabbed the back of his collar and yanked as hard as I could. "Leave her alone!"

The man spun, seeming to notice me for the first time. "Fuck off." He turned back to Gina. I grabbed his arm, and this time he shoved me hard. I fell flat on my rump. The air escaped me in a rush, and my chest tightened painfully. He slammed the passenger door shut and circled to the driver side while I sat in the dirt trying to catch my breath. It was when he got the door open and situated himself in the driver's seat that Noah fired a round of buckshot into the open car door.

"Let her go!" Noah demanded, shuffling purposefully toward the truck and leveling his old Winchester M12 at the man.

He raised his hands in the air. "You shot my car!"

Gina scrambled out of the truck and helped me gently to my feet. She called to Noah, "He took my purse."

The man called from inside the truck. "She works for me. It's my money. She stole it."

"Hand it over," Noah said, circling cautiously until he was only a couple feet away from the man.

"She's nothing but a titty dancer," the man said incredulously. He emptied the purse onto the passenger's seat and threw the empty purse out the window. "There. Take it."

"Give me my money!" Gina yelled. "It's all I have."

Noah said, "Hand it over or I'll shoot."

The man stared at Noah and the gun. He slowly reached down and turned the key in the ignition and gunned the engine, keeping his eyes on Noah the whole while. A smile played slowly across his lips. "You think I'm afraid of an old faggot?" He spit at Noah, hitting the end of the shotgun, and for a moment, I cringed as Noah's finger jiggled on the trigger. But in the end, there was no gunshot, and the man in the truck peeled away, spewing small stones and twigs and dirt behind him.

Noah lowered the shotgun and stared at the ground. Then he shuffled over to me. "You okay?" he asked.

My voice trembled. "I'm okay."

He looked up at Gina. "Sorry I didn't get your money back."

Gina wiped at her eyes and sniffed. "It's okay," she whispered.

"I'm going to go lay down for a while," Noah said. He walked slowly to the lodge. I followed him, feeling the eyes of our guests upon us. Once inside, I gently took the gun from him and helped him into bed. I locked the shotgun back in its cabinet and wandered out to the sunset bench.

★ ★ ★

The sunset bench was forty-feet long and sat halfway down the small slope of hill on the west side of our humble isthmus, positioned to catch the varying hues of salmon and nectarine and crimson that filled the sky and spread like spilled oil over Upper Gull each evening. I hadn't been out to see a sunset in a while, and now I needed to sit and let the rich colors fill and calm me.

Mr. McMahon sat on one end of the bench, his arms spread out on the backrest. His eyes shone. "By golly, that was some excitement. You get that kind of stuff up here a lot?"

I shook my head and chuckled. "Nope. Not much happens up here except maybe somebody has a bit too much to drink, or they play their music too loud, maybe shoot off fireworks in the middle of the night." Then I asked, "Are you enjoying your stay?"

He crossed his legs in front of him, bright white socks pulled up over his calves. "You've got a beautiful place here."

I nodded.

"You got any kids?" he asked.

I looked out at the distant trees, the sun melting into the branches. "Can't say that I have."

McMahon grinned. "Consider yourself lucky."

"Your kids seem nice enough," I offered.

He shrugged. "Ah, heck, they're great. But sometimes a man needs to get away."

We sat in silence for a long while as the world quickly darkened, and before long, a gibbous moon floated in the sky. There was the sound of frogs and the gentle lapping of water against the shore. Muffled voices from the decks and porches of homes edging the lake carried through the air, and soon there was another sound that reached us.

The sound of crying. It came from down the shore, and slowly grew louder. Soon, a figure appeared, accompanying the sound. McMahon and I remained silent as Gina Veale neared, and we watched as she stopped to gaze out over the water. She reached into a pocket. There was the sound of a lighter being engaged, a small burst of flame, and soon the smell of cigarette smoke reached our nostrils. In her other hand, a beer can glistened with condensation. She wore shorts, her yellow tank top and flip-flops. She passed by, oblivious to our presence, and soon the darkness swallowed her.

McMahon broke our silence. "Poor girl," he said. "Poor girl."

That night I lay in bed next to Noah, my arm draped over his sleeping form. When I finally fell asleep, it was deep and hard and dreamless until the sound of an outboard motor pulled me back. I sat up and listened. The boat traveled fast through the narrows, and soon after it passed, waves slapped angrily against the pilings, and the moored boats knocked and thudded against the docks.

"Damn kids," I mumbled and fell back to sleep.

★ ★ ★

The next morning, I noticed the lock on the pump hadn't been attached. Inside the shop, the gas meter was still on. A pending sale waited on the register. I quickly opened the cash drawer and checked the neat piles of money. It seemed to all be there. But in order to unlock the pump, a key was needed, and the key was below.

In all the commotion of the previous night, had I forgotten to lock up the pump? I tried mentally to go through the motions of the night before, but I'd locked up the pump so many nights for so many years, the same act over and over that it came back as one blurred act, and I could not distinguish last night from any other. Getting as bad as Noah, I thought.

The shop door opened. Regal and Blanchard, the two fishermen, walked in, dressed for a day of fishing. The sun was minutes away from bleeding over the horizon, and the sky was a hazy peach.

"Did you hear anything last night?" Blanchard asked.

"Like what?" I asked.

Regal elbowed his buddy. "Jim here is always hearing things."

"I heard a boat speed through the narrows in the middle of the night," I offered. "But other than that…"

Blanchard shrugged. "Thought I heard someone yelp. Like a short scream, kinda."

"Can't say I heard anything like that."

The fishermen paid for one of the fourteen-foot Lund boats, and I signed out number four, but I'd be damned if I could find the key. I crossed out the number on the rental agreement and wrote in a 'three'. At least that key was there. Wouldn't be the first time something around here hadn't been put back in its proper place.

I escorted the fishermen out to the boats, carrying a pair of life-vests for them while they carried the rest of their gear.

Not only was the key to boat number four missing, but the boat was gone as well.

"Noah! Damn it," I muttered.

I assured the fishermen that they needn't worry, and got them on their way. I stomped up to the shop. Noah stood at the register, yawning and scratching his chest. "Morning," he said.

I scowled at him. "Number four is gone."

"What d'ya mean?"

"I mean someone stole it."

"You sure?"

It wasn't the first time one of the boats was taken. They normally ended up along the shore, victim of a joyride. Sometimes the borrowers were even kind enough to sneak them back to the dock.

"I'll call the sheriff," I sighed. As I called, Noah stepped out of the shop, and came back in soon after.

"The girl's gone."

"What girl?"

"You know. The titty dancer."

"Her name's Gina," I scolded. "But what do you mean she's gone?"

"Her door was open a crack. I looked in and she's not there."

I called back the sheriff to tell him to forget about it; we'd figured out where the boat was. The dancer's car was still parked outside and her belongings were still here, so we figured she probably checked the boat out herself.

"She's just out for a ride," I told the sheriff, relieved. "She'll show up soon enough."

★ ★ ★

I stood on the shore staring out at the water lilies, the heads of turtles poking up now and then for a peak at the rising sun. Benny, the foul-mouthed turtle boy, paddled up to the dock thirty minutes later, the floor of his boat crawling with turtles.

"Sons of bitches are fidgety today," he said.

"That right? You want the usual?"

Benny carefully scanned the water's surface. "I'm needing about a dozen more of these bastards before the races today. What the hell's wrong with them? Hey, can I get a Dew and a pack of gum?" he asked, holding up two ones but keeping his eyes on the lake. "Come on, you bastards," he whispered to the still water.

I pointed to the east side of the isthmus where the water lilies lay drenched with sun. "Seems to be a bunch of the bastards over there," I said.

I trudged back up to the shop and got his bubblegum and soda, and by the time I came back to the dock, Benny had maneuvered his canoe among the bright green lily pads, nudging them gently aside with his paddle. His method of turtle entrapment was simple, yet effective. Once he was near enough, he'd stealthily slip his paddle beneath an unsuspecting turtle and scoop the thing up and into his boat before it had time to figure out what had happened. But now he seemed to concentrate on something; a pair of turtle heads poking up next to his boat. They were still and he was still and I wondered what he was waiting for. All he had to do was scoop the things up, and he'd have two for the price of one.

Benny swallowed. He backed up quickly, the boat wobbling violently with the sudden movement. He stood, pointing at the turtle heads, and sat down hard when the boat threatened to tip.

I waved to him. "You all right? Benny?"

He grabbed his paddle and shoved it into the water, back-paddling with frantic strokes, trying to turn the canoe around. I looked closer at the turtles he'd left behind, realizing they hadn't moved this whole time. I squinted at them against the nectarine sun.

"Shit," Benny said. "Shit, shit, shit."

I barely heard him as it dawned on me that maybe they weren't the docile heads of turtles, after all. As a matter of fact, the more I stared at them, the more they looked like a pair of fingers reaching out above the water's placid surface.

"There's someone in there," Benny gasped. "Some lady. I saw her down there. Some lady."

I helped him out of his canoe, and he kneeled on the dock, staring out at the vegetation where the fingers poked out.

"Noah!" I hollered up to the shop. "Call the sheriff. Tell him to get down here as fast as he can."

★ ★ ★

It was Gina. A diver was called to retrieve her body from the lake and search along the rocky bottom and among the green stalks of lily for evidence. An anchor had been tied around her waist, but the water was only five feet deep where she'd been dropped, and her fingers were just long enough to protrude from the surface.

I talked to a deputy about the man from the strip club who'd come for his money, and who tried to take her with him. I was angry at not calling them earlier when the incident had happened. I gave a description of the man and of his truck, and Noah, amazingly, had remembered the license plate number (perhaps because it was B88BS). I also told them about the missing boat, and the boat I'd heard speeding through the narrows in the middle of the night. Was it our boat?

They questioned Mr. McMahon and the fishermen and the newlyweds, and they didn't have much else to add, other than the short, sharp scream Blanchard thought he'd heard. Mrs. Perry thought she might've heard a scream, too, or maybe it was a grunt, she wasn't really sure.

By the time they were done taking everyone's statements, the sheriff received a call on his radio that they'd apprehended the strip club owner. They found her money on him, and he was still dressed in the clothes he'd worn the previous night.

★ ★ ★

I tried to put it together. The strip club owner. He must've driven here in the middle of the night. Killed her. Put her in the boat and dumped her.

But he already had her money.

And why go through the trouble of hauling her to the other side of the isthmus to put her in a boat in order to take her back to the Bass Lake side, when that's where her cabin was? Wouldn't it have been easier to just carry her to that spot? Less risk of getting caught by someone out for a breath of fresh air?

But maybe she'd run from him, run to the Upper Gull side and that's where he killed her. So he put her in the boat, and…

But still, he had her money.

Maybe it was about more than money. Maybe he was a jilted lover, or…

But no, he said she worked for him. And he hadn't acted like a jilted lover, had he?

While I thought through all this, images kept running through my head, images of all the young girls who had stayed here, all the girls I could remember, trying to conjure a face from the past and reconcile it with Gina Veale's world weary visage.

★ ★ ★

The next day, one of the residents on nearby Roy Lake called. Rosy Smith. She lived with her aging father in one of the many beautiful large homes that kept popping up all over these lakes. She said that one of our boats was moored on their dock. She said it had appeared the previous day, and she wondered when someone would come back for it, then noticed it had our name and phone number on it, so finally decided to call us. I drove down to their property with Noah, where we met the sheriff and one of his deputies.

Our Lund boat. The anchor was missing. No surprise there. But what did surprise me was the strong, familiar smell that wafted up from the boat's interior.

It wasn't until Noah and I drove back to the lodge that I placed the smell and realized what it meant.

★ ★ ★

Noah and I sat on the long wooden sunset bench facing Upper Gull and watched as the sun disappeared behind the trees, turning the sky a brilliant pink. I promised myself that I would do this more often, because this is what this bench was put here for, and I lived here, and why shouldn't I do this every evening? Besides, who knew how many more sunsets were left for me. Or for Noah. I let go of his hand when I heard footsteps clunk across the deck's wooden planks.

Mr. McMahon nodded at us, and sat down about five feet from Noah. He squinted into the sunset and sighed. I watched him a moment, then asked, "Why did you folks decide to stay?"

"What do you mean? We registered for a week."

Soft, golden light dripped among the distant branches and spread like a slow fire across the water's surface. I kept my eyes on the lake. "Why did you do it?"

Noah slipped his hand back in mine and squeezed gently.

McMahon chuckled like I was some crazy old man. I looked at him. Stared at him. Stared until his smile faded. He said quietly, "You think I killed her?" He twisted the wedding ring on his finger.

Now Noah stared at him, too. "It doesn't really matter what we think," he said gently. "I'm sure they'll find plenty to make a case against you."

McMahon looked at us incredulously. His mouth opened and closed like a landed fish. "You don't—" he started. His head shook. "You don't know anything."

We watched him silently. Waiting.

He tugged one white sock up over his bare calf. Said quietly, "I tried to help her. That's all." He stood up slowly, brushing imaginary dirt from his shorts. He turned to look back at the cabins and sighed. Then he chuckled. "Why waste my breath on a couple old queens like you, anyway?"

Noah's voice shook. "Try us."

McMahon said, "I thought she could use some money."

I frowned. "So you gave it to her out of the kindness of your heart?"

Noah grunted next to me.

"Like I said, you two wouldn't understand." He sat back down on the edge of his seat and rocked back and forth, elbows on knees, hands cupped together. "Geez," he muttered. "Jesus." He blinked. The sun danced delicately on ripples of water stirred up by a cooling breeze. Finally he looked up at us. His voice caught in his throat. "My wife found us," he said, waving a hand at the Lunds pulled up on the shore. "We were in one of your boats. Mary's usually a heavy sleeper, but that night…" He shook his head. "She found us in the boat, and she just picked up the anchor and hit her over the head. It happened so fast."

His words sunk in, and my heart seemed like it had filled with a thick sap. Noah leaned back and turned his face up to the sky, his mouth hanging open, his tongue smoothing over his teeth.

"We had to get rid of her and the boat," McMahon said. "We took the boat out and tied the anchor to her. I didn't realize the water was so shallow. I tried to sink the damn boat, too, but do you know how hard that is? To sink a boat? We tried filling it with water, and I tried, but I just couldn't do it. So Mary decided we had to at least clean it, hopefully get rid of any evidence. So she went and got some Pine-Sol, and we scrubbed it out."

That's what I had smelled in the boat. The Pine-Sol.

"We each took a boat and followed each other, left one boat on someone's dock and sped back here with the other one." He looked at each of us in turn. "It was an accident. I was just trying to help her." He turned his palms up. "I just thought she could use the money."

"Where's your wife," I asked, realizing that I hadn't seen her or his kids all day.

"They went back home. She couldn't stand to look at me, and she took the kids back home and left me here without a damn car." He chuckled nervously. "So if either of you guys are heading to Duluth…."

Neither Noah nor I smiled.

"Look," McMahon said. "That man they arrested—that thug—he deserves to be in prison. Right? He should be there. Not me. Not Mary. Besides, that girl, Mary probably did her a favor. Look where she was headed. What kind of life was she going to lead?"

Noah and I slowly stood, our hands still together, and we walked past McMahon, heading up the small slope of hill to the lodge. We went inside, and I held onto the screen door to stop it from slamming, and then Noah held me, and my face was on his shoulder and I couldn't stop the tears. Partly for the loss of Ms. Veale's life, but mostly because I had a sudden memory.

Gina Veale when she was seven.

I remembered.

I remembered.

Her standing on the shore while her mother and father waited, and she set down the turtles, one at a time, tears streaming down her soft cheeks as she waved goodbye to the slow, ambling creatures.

I remembered.

She looked up and saw me watching her, and she looked at me questioningly as if asking me to save them for her, to keep them safe, and I remembered.

I remembered smiling at her and winking, as if to say, Of course I will.

Was it only the first of so many lies and disappointments she'd have to endure?

And then she was gone and the memory was gone, and I could not stop the tears.

Finally, Noah pulled away from me. "I'll call the sheriff," he said. He reached out and gently rubbed the back of my neck. His forehead touched mine. "Let's get up early tomorrow," he said. "Let's watch the sunrise together."

I nodded. Yes, I silently agreed. We should watch the sunrise and the sunset as often as we could. Who knew how many we'd have left?

Deborah Woodworth

Deborah Woodworth, who grew up in the warmth of Southern Ohio, finds Minnesota winters conducive to the contemplation of murder. Her first mystery short story, "Waltz of the Loons," appeared in The Silence of the Loons *anthology (2005). Jens Johansson, a northern Minnesota police chief, makes his second appearance in "The Moose Whisperer."*

After a 1991 visit to the Herb House in the last remaining Shaker community—Sabbathday Lake, Maine—Woodworth was inspired to create Sister Rose Callahan, sleuth and Eldress of a dwindling Shaker village in Depression-era Kentucky. Death of a Winter Shaker *was published in 1997, followed by five more Sister Rose adventures.* Publishers Weekly *called the award-winning Sister Rose mysteries "a first-rate series; warmhearted, richly detailed, and completely enthralling." Woodworth is currently finishing a seventh book in the series.*

*Woodworth lives in St. Paul with her husband of nineteen years, Norm Schiferl, environmental planner and garden design consultant. She can be contacted at **deborahwoodworth@comcast.net**.*

The Moose Whisperer

Deborah Woodworth

L ast night I dreamed again of dying.
I haven't had a dream like that in months. Then it was Angela
dying, or I think it was. That would make sense—she'd hurt me, so
I wanted her to die. It worries me that I can't remember.

When the dreams came before, I stopped them by sleeping
only four hours a night. Now I awaken without an alarm, even
though the nights are long and cold up here. Tonight I'll sleep two
hours, no more. Anything to stop the dreams.

Less sleep means more time with the animals. The deer are
now at ease in my presence. I track the herd through the snow, then
stand quietly near them until they allow me to come closer. Last
night their leader, a powerful buck with battle-scarred hide, came
to the edge of the frozen lake and spoke with me. I warned him not
to trust other humans. He nodded and pointed his nose at a healed
wound on his back where a hunter's rifle grazed him.

I used to hunt, didn't I? When I was young?

★ ★ ★

Police Chief Jens Johansson lifted one resistant eyelid. What woke
him up this time? Couldn't blame his dog, Mutt, who was sleeping
on a blanket on the floor. Did the phone ring? Then he remembered he wasn't back home in Loon River, where the nighttime
ring of a phone meant hustling to a crime scene. He was way up in
the North Woods, staying at the Snowy Pine Lodge. His cabin had
no phone, and the Lodge was too remote for cell phone service.

Jens clicked through the rest of his nocturnal inventory. It was dark, not time to get up. Noise wasn't the problem, except for Mutt's snoring, and that was comforting. The bedroom windows, sealed against the February winds, shut out the sounds of woodland creatures fighting to the death for food or dominance.

However, a more personal call of nature was making itself heard. Second time that night. Maybe he could ignore it, go back to sleep. He hated rousting those dark, furry little critters—voles were they?—that inhabited his bathroom and scurried off to who knows where when he flipped on the light. Made him wonder what lived under his bed.

This was not his idea of a mid-winter vacation. Well, he'd come here as a favor to his nephew, Petey, and his wife Phyllis, who had just inherited the Lodge and needed winter visitors to keep the place going. Besides, Jens hated traveling alone. If Klara had lived, they'd be in Hawaii now. Bermuda, maybe.

In the end, Jens threw on his robe and answered the call, cursing the process of aging and enlarged prostates in particular. He took Mutt along to chase off the bathroom beasties.

Urgent mission accomplished, Jens was fully awake. "Insult to injury," he announced to Mutt, who'd claimed the couch in the small living room. "Bette Davis had it right, getting old isn't for sissies. Might as well accept my fate and brew some coffee."

By his second cup of extra-strong French roast, Jens felt more at peace. He thought about taking Mutt on a stimulating walk through the woods, stopping to marvel at the winter beauty of Glass Lake, maybe frozen all the way to Canada. On the other hand, his cabin was warm, and the large living-room window offered a view of the lake through the trees.

All of life's decisions should be so easy. Easy as krumkake, as Klara used to say.

Jens turned off the kitchen light and drew open the heavy living room curtain. After a mighty stretch, Mutt hopped off the couch to join him. A few feet away, a startled deer performed a high dancing leap into the woods. Held back by glass, Mutt whimpered his frustration.

Jens felt a sigh go through him at the sight of Glass Lake, its sharp beauty softened by the full moon. A herd of deer, twenty or more, wandered across its frozen surface. Something else was there, too. At first, Jens thought it must be a tree stump rising out of the snowy shore, but then it moved. It was a person, had to be, edging onto the lake.

The deer didn't seem alarmed by the approaching figure, though a huge buck watched him. Jens could see only the man's back. He was sure-footed, though, not a stumbling city fellow playing weekend north-woodsman.

A small doe separated from the herd and walked toward the man. "Well, I'll be danged," Jens said. "Will you look at that?" He'd begun talking to himself after Klara died, though he insisted he was just keeping Mutt informed.

The doe hesitated, then ventured close enough to touch. Her head lowered until it was hidden behind the man. Jens couldn't see enough to be certain, but it sure looked like she might be eating out of his hand.

"I'd better talk to Petey about this," Jens said. "Those deer are too tame for their own good. That poor girl will get herself shot or eaten by a wolf if she doesn't wise up." The thought made him sad. Hunting for food was one thing, he'd done it his whole life and, to be truthful, enjoyed it. But deer shouldn't be taught to trust, that didn't seem right. It was like killing a pet.

"Gets my dander all in a bunch," Jens said, giving Mutt's ears a fond scratch. "Never mind waiting for Petey, let's go have a talk with that guy."

Dressed in four layers, Jens hooked Mutt's leash on his collar. "Sorry you can't run free, boy, but that's how it is." Mutt had inherited good manners from the Labrador side of his ancestry, but the terrier part couldn't be trusted.

The high winds had quieted, but the cold felt like a razor slicing Jens's exposed skin. He wrapped his wool scarf around his face, leaving only his eyes uncovered. Beyond the light from his cabin window, tall pines blocked the moonlight and darkness closed around him. The uneven terrain was booby-trapped with patches of ice and crusty snow, so he had to concentrate on each step. Mutt, with his canine senses, didn't understand the problem and yanked insistently on his leash, straining to run.

"Some cop I am," Jens muttered. "Can't even remember to bring a flashlight."

By the time they emerged from the woods and could see the lake, both the deer and their human friend had disappeared.

"Well, at least I didn't break any bones. Come on, boy, might as well walk the shore and watch the sunrise."

★ ★ ★

I've stopped dreaming altogether now. Slept like the dead for two hours but needed the alarm to wake up. The buzzing shot me through a world of shadows, vaguely familiar, but they went by too fast for me to grab. I heard cries of pain, like animals dying. Are they the animals I used to kill?

Luckily, this journal tracks my days and reminds me why I am here. The animals help—the moose and deer, and the wolves, even the squirrels, in their own way. They soften the world for me.

★ ★ ★

Jens had some serious digesting to do before bed, having consumed enough wine and walleye to nourish two men his size, which was considerable. Yielding to the seduction of a spitting fire, he sank into one of the overstuffed armchairs in the Lodge's common room. His plan for the evening was simple. An hour or so of staring into the dancing flames, then back to his cabin and bed.

"Hey, Uncle Jens, Phyl tells me you went skulking after our moose whisperer in the middle of the night." Petey Granger landed on the armchair next to Jens and stretched his legs toward the fireplace. "Just can't stop being a cop, can you, even on vacation?"

Tired after a day of trudging through the woods, Jens was in no mood for teasing from his cocky young nephew. He gave Petey his best glaring frown. However, Petey was family and not impressed.

"Tasty walleye," Jens said, hoping to redirect the conversation.

"Noticed you scraped the plate clean," Petey said, with a smirk. "I told Phyl, take it as a compliment. Uncle Jens knows his walleye."

Petey seemed to be in rare form, irritating yet somehow charming.

"Seriously, though," Petey said. "There's no mystery about the guy you saw feeding the deer. We think of him as our very own moose whisperer. He's got an amazing way with all the animals. Phyl said you were worried about the deer becoming too trusting. Funny thing is, they seem more careful around other people once they've gotten to know Bjorn."

"Bjorn?"

"Bjorn Wolfquist," Petey said. "He owns the farthest cabin out. Back in the woods, real secluded."

Watching Petey bounce up to throw more logs on the fire, Jens thought of Klara. Petey was her sister's boy, youngest of five. He had his mother's fair hair, but Klara's sturdy build and quickness.

"I never actually met the guy face to face," Petey said, dropping back in his chair. "Neither has Phyl."

"And you don't think that's odd?"

Petey shrugged. "A guy's entitled to his privacy. Especially when he has paid a bundle for it. He bought the cabin from Gran for about five times what it's worth, and every month we get a check for his meals that pays half our food bill for the whole lodge. He's the reason we could keep this place in the family."

Jens felt his cop antennae poke up. "Anyone who pays that much for privacy must have quite a story to tell."

"See, there, I knew you'd stick your nose in," Petey said.

A couple of red-cheeked, wool-bundled guests entered the common room, stomping their feet to shake off the caked snow. Petey leaned toward Jens and lowered his voice. "Look, Uncle Jens, the extra income we get from this guy is what's keeping us afloat right now. Don't scare him off, okay? He isn't some crazed psychopath on the lam, he couldn't be, not and be so gentle with the animals. He just doesn't like people."

"Can't deny I've often felt that way myself," Jens said. Petey and Phyllis' plight had triggered that blend of compassion and guilt so often traded among close relatives. Any other time, Jens would have offered financial help, but Klara's final illness had drained their savings.

"It was rough when we first took over this place, while Gran was dying." Petey's right leg began bouncing up and down, a nervous habit he'd had since boyhood. "Nobody in the family knew how sick she'd been. You know Gran, she wouldn't admit to a headache, let alone cancer. She tried to keep track of everything, but the finances got away from her. She was close to losing the Lodge when Wolfquist showed up. Gran's the only one who ever met him, back when he and his wife stayed as guests. Pretty girl, Gran said, much younger than him."

"So Wolfquist wasn't always a recluse."

"Guess not," Petey said. "Gran said he had a real head for figures. Offered to go over the books with her, straighten things out so she could make best use of what money was left. When he saw how far in the red she was, he proposed a deal. Him and his wife wanted a place to be completely private, where no one would bother them. He worked in the Cities and just needed solitude sometimes. He wanted to buy the cabin outright, offered more than Gran needed to get out of debt, plus a generous check for food and basic supplies. A check came every month, even though the Wolfquists never came back while Gran was alive. In exchange, Gran promised they'd never be disturbed, even by staff."

Very, very odd, Jens thought. He kept it to himself, though, to keep Petey talking.

"Gran signed some papers and handed over the key to the cabin. Wolfquist delivered a cashier's check the next day. Gran showed us the paper and made us promise to keep up her end of the deal after she was gone. A couple months after we buried Gran, we found a printed note thumb-tacked to the back door saying Wolfquist was back and insisting on complete privacy."

"You and Phyl, you've never even tried to see his face?"

Petey's habitual grin, big and infectious, reappeared. "If we broke our word, Gran would come barreling down that stairway from heaven and make us both eat lutefisk. Wolfquist asked for some supplies and one meal a day, at dinnertime. Phyl leaves everything outside the front door, covered up so the wildlife won't get to it."

"No wife, eh?" Jens's mind raced, the way it always did when clues began to collect. Could be the wife left him or died young, which might turn a man into a hermit. Or it could be more sinister. Jens knew he couldn't return home to Loon River without knowing the rest of Bjorn Wolfquist's story. He'd figure it out for himself, keep Petey out of it; he'd only fuss.

★ ★ ★

After breakfast the next morning, Jens retrieved his truck from the Lodge parking lot. Petey and Phyllis were so busy they wouldn't miss him. Jens drove until his cell phone picked up service, at which point he pulled to the side of the road and dialed a Minneapolis number.

"That you, Ben?" Jens asked, when he finally got through to his former partner, Ben Walsh. "Now you're a lieutenant, I thought I'd have to sign over my dog just to get through to you."

"Not a chance. That mangy mutt is all yours. So how are you, Jens?"

Cell phone service being what it was, Jens wasted no time in pleasantries. He filled Ben in briefly, adding, "Here's my question: In the last couple years, have there been any disappearances involving a wealthy Twin Cities man, maybe in a financial profession of some sort? There might have been a wife and/or mistress."

"Funny you should ask."

"Speak. Cell phones run out of juice, you know."

"Age has not granted you patience," Ben said. "Anyway, yeah, we had a case about a year ago. Guy named Erik Androwski, an investment banker with his own firm in downtown Minneapolis. Wife named Angela Androwski. The mistress was Marta, can't recall the last name. A twenty-something blond, very ambitious. All three disappeared at the same time. Made the front pages of the *Star Tribune*; I'm surprised you didn't know about it." The connection went silent for a moment. "Sorry, Jens, I wasn't thinking."

Jens's wife Klara had died the previous year. The newspapers had piled up for months before he finally carted them all to the recycling center. He pushed the memory aside.

"Anyway, I supervised that case, so if you've got anything, tell me. Want me to send somebody up there? I hate not closing a case."

"Not sure," Jens said. "Give me the background and I'll think about it."

"Okay, here's the short version. Erik Androwski was a forty-year-old hot shot making piles of money. Grew up in Nordeast Minneapolis and never forgot his humble beginnings. He and his wife hosted charity events, did some volunteer work together, contributed thousands for the children's leukemia wing at Westdale Hospital. They kept a couple animal shelters afloat almost single-handedly."

"I'm guessing there's another side to the story," Jens said.

"Right," Ben said. "The year before his disappearance, Androwski began to change. Spent less time on good deeds and more on making money. His financial records disappeared with him, but we suspected he'd been stashing money away offshore. Only had about fifty thousand in the joint savings account.

"We figured he and the mistress had been planning an exit for some time, but when the wife disappeared, too, we wondered if maybe she'd found out, and he killed her. Two registered guns, both missing, but no signs of violence at the house. They owned an Acura, which we never found, and a Lincoln Navigator, still in the garage and clean. The mistress's car was found abandoned at the Twin Cities airport. Neighbors in New Brighton didn't notice a thing, thought the Androwskis were the perfect couple. They didn't know about the mistress; we got that from his secretary."

"Describe Androwski."

Ben laughed. "It's a good thing Erik was rich. Short and stout, dark hair, condescending to anyone he didn't like. On the other hand, his secretary said he was kind to people he did like, and he didn't care if they were rich or poor.

The wife, Angela, was his high school sweetheart. Quiet little thing, dark hair, pretty in a girl-next-door way. Guess she didn't stand a chance against a blond bulldozer like Marta."

The cell went dead for a few seconds. Jens checked the battery symbol and realized he was down to two bars. "Ben, my cell's about to die. One more question: Did Androwski actually like kids and animals?"

"Couldn't say for sure. They didn't have kids. We did find half a bag of dog food in the house but no abandoned dog. Why? Never mind, save your cell. Hey, I'll be off this weekend; what if I come up there?"

"I'll let you know," Jens said.

★ ★ ★

Jens went to bed fully clothed, so when he awakened for his two o'clock bathroom run, all he had to do was slip on boots and a parka. This time he remembered to grab a flashlight and, just in case, his service revolver.

"Sorry, buddy," he said to Mutt, who was waiting by the front door. "You're a fine watchdog and that's the problem. Can't afford to have you start barking."

Mutt whimpered and lay down with his head on his paws. Jens scratched his ears. "Nice try, but no rice," he said, borrowing one of Klara's signature food phrases.

Jens walked just inside the woods so he could stay hidden while keeping Glass Lake in sight. About the time he began to wonder about frostbite, a herd of deer wandered onto the frozen lake. Within minutes, a now-familiar, well-bundled figure emerged from the tree cover and crept toward them.

Moonlight reflected on the ice gave Jens a good view of the scene. Wolfquist seemed to be on the short side, though it was hard to tell much more. A scarf and a thick hat, flaps down, hid his head and neck. He seemed sure-footed as he approached the buck, who stood his ground and watched. When they were no more than a few feet apart, Wolfquist slowly reached into his coat pocket, then withdrew his hand and held it out toward the buck. With his other hand, he lowered the scarf from his face.

Jens stepped beyond the tree cover, hoping to get a glimpse of Wolfquist's face. At once the buck skittered to the side and looked toward the woods. Jens ducked behind a tree as the man covered his face and spun around.

Early in his career, Jens had worked a few years in the Minneapolis Police Department, where he'd honed his surveillance skills. A couple decades in Loon River had turned him rusty. Feeling old, Jens headed back to his cabin and a few hours of sleep. Getting sloppy, he thought, pulling the covers over his head. Losing my edge. Mutt wasn't supposed to sleep on the bed, but he hopped up anyway. For once, Jens pretended not to notice.

★ ★ ★

Can't sleep. Someone watched me tonight as I spoke to the deer. The buck saw him and said he was spying on us. I know who it is. It's that man Angela ran off with, that trucker from Canada. Somehow he found out I was here. The lake is frozen, he must have walked across it to find me. But why?

Angela must be tired of him. He doesn't have enough money. He thinks she has come back to me, so he has come looking for her. If he kills me, he can take everything I have and get Angela back.

I must be on the alert at all times. From now on, I take the pistol with me.

★ ★ ★

The next morning, Jens awakened at 1:45 and set out again, determined to do a better job. This time he wore extra socks and carried a small pair of binoculars. Taking a different path through the woods, he reached a wooded spot closer to the lake. Within minutes, the herd appeared. For a while, Jens lost himself in the crystalline beauty of the scene, the animals so sure and graceful they seemed to glide along the snow-sprinkled ice.

By 3:00 a.m., cold had penetrated three pairs of wool socks and the deer had lost their appeal. No sign of their human friend. Jens figured he must have spooked the fellow into changing his nighttime pattern. Maybe he'd stayed in bed.

Bed sounded good. On the other hand, his vacation nights were dwindling, and Jens wasn't one to quit. He followed the gravel road leading past the Lodge and into woods denser than those close to the lake.

Jens was so intent on listening for human sounds, the distant call of a moose barely registered in his awareness. However, the sound of undergrowth being crushed by a thousand pounds of wild animal got his full attention. He had great respect and appreciation for moose. With a moose, you knew where you stood. Not too close.

The noise intensified, then stopped. Instead of another call, Jens heard a quieter sound—a murmuring human voice. Without light, he wouldn't be able to see the owner of the voice, but he knew who it had to be.

Praise the lord and pass the pancakes, Jens still had acute hearing. He huddled behind a tree and listened. From the few words Jens could make out, man and moose were discussing human perfidy and the difficulty of finding food in a northern Minnesota winter. At one point, Jens could have sworn Wolfquist was asking after the moose's wife—wives, rather—and children.

Finally, Wolfquist's voice took on a sterner tone. The warning to "be careful" came through clearly. The crunch of boots on snow indicated he was leaving—not, thankfully, in Jens's direction. However, a more substantial crunch announced that the moose, too, was on the move. Right toward Jens.

Running seemed a bad idea. He could slip on the ice and be trampled by a huge, panicked animal that'd just been reminded to distrust humans. Even if Jens managed to escape, the ruckus would surely alert the creature's human protector.

Maybe the moose would pass by without noticing him. Jens held his breath, sent out a silent but urgent Lutheran prayer, and waited. The moose appeared, so near that Jens's peripheral vision caught the gigantic flat antlers, with a spread the size of a man. Under them, the long lugubrious face. Next appeared the front legs, like sturdy tree trunks. The animal paused, lifting his nose to test the air.

Jens thought maybe he should have made that prayer nondenominational.

The moose's heavy head swung toward Jens, who, against all reason, turned to look at him. Large brown eyes took in the human presence. Jens forced himself to look down, signaling his inferior status. The moose emitted a grunting sound, which Jens understood to be disparaging, and shuffled off. Just before he disappeared, the animal raised his magnificent antlers and sent a call into the woods.

Jens slid down the tree bark and thanked the gods, all of them this time.

★ ★ ★

Writing this at night by candlelight. I can see in the dark like a mountain lion. Do moose see in the dark? I'll ask my friend. Last night the moose called to me that the man was near. I don't even know his name, the man who has come to kill me.

Haven't slept for two nights, don't need sleep anymore, just cat naps when my eyes close on their own for a few seconds. My body no longer needs food, either. The meals come as always, but I give them to the animals. It's a tough winter for foraging, they need it and I don't.

I wait and watch. They plan to kill me, but first they want to make me suffer, to go insane. The torture is Angela's idea. She has become someone I never knew, someone so cruel she is no longer human.

I saw Angela. Earlier tonight I couldn't sleep, thought I'd fetch some wood for a fire. Didn't bother with lights, I know the way. I'd left the curtains open. She was staring through the window at me. At first I thought it must be a hungry deer with those black eyes, but the face was hers. I grabbed the pistol and ran outside, but she was gone, evaporated into the air.

★ ★ ★

Jens went to sleep right after an early, light supper and got up at midnight. Instead of searching the woods, he hid among the trees crowding around Wolfquist's cabin. He'd witnessed enough moose whispering; now he wanted to do some solid detective work. If Wolfquist followed his nightly schedule, he'd be heading out soon, which would give Jens his opportunity.

Through Wolfquist's open living room curtain, he could see the flickering of a candle. Did the man never sleep? Jens waited, keeping still no matter how cold he got. It was imperative that Wolfquist not suspect his presence.

After about fifteen minutes, the cabin door flew open. Jens just had time to slip behind the thick trunk of a fir tree. Inching his head around enough to watch, he saw that Wolfquist wore a jacket, but no parka, and his head was uncovered. The hair looked dark, though it was hard to be sure without more light. Jens didn't dare step out far enough to see the man's face, but he recognized the shape of a small gun in his hand.

Wolfquist swiveled around, agitated, as if looking for someone. Apparently satisfied no one was there, he went back inside his cabin.

Don't tell me I've blown it again, Jens thought. Or does this guy have animal instincts himself? All he could do was wait and see. Which he did, for another fifteen minutes or so, until Wolfquist again emerged. This time he was bundled up.

Wolfquist headed toward Glass Lake. Jens waited a few minutes, then scooted to the cabin door. Being a police officer and, more important, a former boy scout, Jens had brought along his lock picks. He wasn't above some discreet breaking and entering if it helped find a killer. Klara used to say he tracked criminals like a beagle scenting a steak.

Once inside, Jens whipped the living room curtains shut and shone his flashlight around the cabin. It was set up like his own, but remarkably bare. He noted empty dishes piled on a tray in the kitchen, a small bottle of milk in the refrigerator, a tin coffeepot on the stove, and a Folgers can on the counter. No television or radio, no computer or any other electronic signs of modernity.

The bedroom had the feel of an empty hotel room. No smell of dirty linens, as if it wasn't used much. The bed was made, and Wolfquist's few spare clothes, neatly folded, filled only one drawer. Jens removed a pair of frayed jeans and held them up. He recognized the rugged, generic style sold at Glass Lake Outfitters. He checked the waist size—thirty. If these belonged to Erik Androwski, he had slimmed down considerably in the past year. He ordered only one meal a day; that plus nights spent outdoors could sure take the weight off fast. Jens refolded the jeans and replaced them.

In the bathroom he found one towel, a damp washcloth, a sliver of soap, and a comb. The rusty metal medicine cabinet over the sink was empty except for a toothbrush, a small tube of toothpaste, and a box of Band-Aids. Not even an aspirin. Either Wolfquist never got sick, or he ignored pain. As Jens closed the cabinet door, he realized it had no mirror. In fact, there wasn't a single mirror in the bathroom. He did a quick check of the other rooms. No mirrors anywhere. A man who cannot bear to see his own face?

Jens returned to the kitchen and searched the drawers. Aside from the most basic kitchen utensils and one set of tinware, he found nothing.

The living room held only a small couch, one chair, and a table. On the table, a chipped saucer held a white candle melted into the shape of a flowing volcano. Jens sat on the chair facing the candle and stared at it. Is this all he does, stare at a burning candle? Where are the books, the newspapers? There had to be something, somewhere. Jens let his gaze roam over the room. Finally, next to the fireplace, he spotted a wide green strap poking out from under a pile of firewood. He studied the arrangement of the wood before moving it, piece by piece, onto the floor. Underneath he found a battered backpack. Without altering its position, he unzipped the top, reached inside, and felt a book. Only it wasn't a book; it was a journal with a hard, black cover and a Bic ballpoint wedged inside.

Jens checked his watch. He'd been quick, so far only about five minutes in the cabin. He opened the journal and began to read the story of a man betrayed by the woman he loved and trusted. At first, the handwriting was small and cramped, showing tight control. Gradually it grew sloppier, words galloping across the pages. Jens reached the last entry, written while he had stood outside watching the cabin.

"Well, well," Jens said softly. "Angela's ghost has appeared. I'd say our suspect is losing more than weight." Still, something bothered him. He couldn't put his finger on it, so he left it to compost in the back of his mind.

When he'd finished, Jens left the cabin precisely as he'd found it and went out to find Wolfquist.

★ ★ ★

Awake all night. I visited the hills where the wolves live and called to them. They assured me all was well, that they were keeping a careful watch. They said that ghosts could not hurt me. Why can't I believe them? The wolves wouldn't lie to me, but they didn't know Angela. She is evil.

★ ★ ★

Jens slept until close to noon the next day. He needed to be clear-headed. Well nourished, too, so he took time for a hot lunch. Slipping out before Petey could corner him, Jens hooked on Mutt's leash, gathered his fully-charged cell phone and a thermos of hot coffee, and set out in his truck. His cop senses were tingling non-stop, and there were preparations to be made.

Once in range, Jens called his old partner again. "The lieutenant took a personal day, said he was driving up north for the weekend," he was told.

"Thanks, that's all I needed to know. If he happens to check in, tell him to make it snappy. I'll leave word for him at the Snowy Pine Lodge."

"Sure thing. You guys have fun."

Darkness would arrive in a few hours, and Jens wanted to be back at the Lodge before then. At the local hardware store, he bought some rope, a strap-on flashlight, and a butane blowtorch, all of which he stowed under a blanket in his truck. By this time, Mutt was whining and bouncing around the cab. Jens knew what that meant. He drove just outside of town and took Mutt for a walk. Just long enough for the necessities.

On his way back to the Lodge, Jens stopped at Glass Lake Outfitters for a sturdy pair of hiking boots with nonskid soles. At the checkout, he grabbed some trail mix, just in case. He splurged on the kind with dried blueberries.

While Mutt watched the white countryside roll by, Jens put the finishing touches on his plan for the night. Climbing an icy incline in the dark was risky for a man his age and size. Good thing he took all those long winter walks back home, he'd need strength and balance.

After finishing Wolfquist's journal the night before, Jens had gone out looking for him. Jens was familiar with the howls and yips of the wolves, so when a human voice called to them, he knew the difference. He'd followed the sound until he saw Wolfquist standing in the moonlight, looking toward a flat area halfway up an icy hill. Wolfquist had lifted his head to the sky and howled. The wolves responded and Wolfquist fell to his knees.

That conversation with the wolves, Jens had a hunch about it. Even the name Wolfquist—could there be a more obvious alias? Wolfquist had formed a deep bond with those wolves. His voice had quivered when he called them, as if he were seeking reassurance. It was a big leap, but what if he had buried his wife's body on that ledge? He could be crazy enough to believe the wolves were watching over the grave.

Instead of relaxing in front of the Lodge fire after dinner, Jens stopped by the front desk to drop off an envelope for Ben Walsh, then headed back to his cabin. He picked up his newly purchased supplies, snapped on Mutt's leash, and headed for the spot where he'd last seen Wolfquist. Mutt seemed to know their purpose was serious; he didn't so much as whimper.

★ ★ ★

I can feel them watching me. Those eyes…. Waiting, infinitely patient, eternally accusing. I can't go out tonight, maybe never again. No one to talk to, not the deer or the moose or my wolves, no one but ghosts. Are they ghosts? Could the wolves be wrong?

I cleaned the shotgun and slid it under the sofa, in case they come for me.

So tired.

★ ★ ★

Jens and Mutt stumbled their way through the woods to the ledge where Wolfquist had howled to the wolves. It was past midnight, but they managed the trip without mishap, mostly because Mutt, his Labrador heritage in ascendance, steered Jens away from ice patches and tree roots.

Jens cleaned off some snow and ice, revealing an area of disturbed ground. "Looks like an animal's been at it," Jens said to Mutt, who was straining at his leash.

"Sorry, boy, not yet." Jens tied the leash around a tree. "You keep an ear open, let me know if anyone is coming."

Jens did a slow sweep of his flashlight across the ledge. Something, probably a wolf, had dug up an area about two feet by four feet, maybe a foot deep. Kneeling to take a closer look, Jens muttered, "No sign of a body, but this sure looks like it could have been a shallow grave. Probably have to wait till spring to find out for sure. However…

Jens blowtorched the area enough to melt the ice and soften the top layer of earth. He untied Mutt and walked him to the hole. "Don't break your claws, boy, just sniff around, see if you can smell anything."

Mutt seemed interested in the bottom of one corner. He looked up at Jens and whimpered. When his master didn't move fast enough, Mutt tried to dig into the frozen dirt.

"Hey, what did I just tell you?" Jens shone his flashlight in the direction of Mutt's scratching. Something was protruding from the hard earth. On closer inspection, it was about half an inch wide, with a diameter that was part round and part straight.

"Looks familiar." As Jens cracked away bits of dirt, using his pocketknife, the object lengthened and began to widen. The flashlight picked up a hint of red fabric.

"Well now," Jens said, "I believe we've got ourselves the bottom of a woman's high-heeled shoe. Interesting."

★ ★ ★

If I can't be outside with the animals, there's nothing left. No reason to go on. Time to end this, even if it ends my life.

I open the curtains. She is there. I'm pretending to sit and write, but I am really moving to the window. She's not the only one who can play at being a ghost.

"What do you want from me?" I ask, being reasonable, smiling. She smiles back. She doesn't know that this is the final battle.

"Tell me what you want." Now I am demanding, powerful. I open my mouth to shout at her, and I hear her voice.

"Sweetheart," I hear her whisper. "Don't you remember?"

"Stop calling me that. I hate it when you call me that."

"I know you do, but it has to be done."

"Go away!" I swing my arm, as if to hit her, and she raises her own arm in self-defense. I lower my arm and stare at her.

"Sweetheart."

"Stop it!" I'm screaming at her. I have to stop that voice, her voice, trying to make me remember.

★ ★ ★

The blast shattered a chunk of the window.

Jens had been keeping watch while he waited for Ben and the police to arrive. He'd taken cover when he saw the appearance of what looked like a shotgun, but he peeked around the tree trunk in time to see glass shards arch in the air and settle on the snow like splintered icicles.

Jens looped Mutt's leash around a tree—loose enough so escape was possible, just in case. "Now stay," he said, in his firmest alpha-dog voice. With a token whimper, Mutt obeyed.

Jens needed to get to the cabin fast; however, running straight for the shattered window didn't seem the brightest choice. He compromised by coming at it sideways, his revolver ready.

As he edged along the front of the cabin, the butt of a shotgun smashed through what remained of the living room window. Jens flattened against the rough log exterior, shielding his face with his arm. When the crackling stopped, Jens lowered his arm to see the gun's barrel emerge through the broken window.

Jens' relief that the shotgun was not pointed at him evaporated in an instant. Apparently his order to stay had expired. Mutt bounded from the woods and loped toward his master. The gun shifted toward Mutt.

Acting on desperate impulse, Jens snatched up a nearby rock and hurled it back toward the tree cover, yelling, "Fetch, boy, fetch!" Mutt executed a leaping turn and raced after the rock.

The shotgun barrel momentarily followed Mutt. Then it swung toward Jens.

"Angela Androwski, you are under arrest for the murders of Erik Androwski and his mistress Marta. You have the right—"

A sound like the keening wail of a wounded wolf interrupted him, and Jens felt a shiver go through him. Tightening his grip on his revolver, he moved closer. Angela Androwski's gaunt face appeared.

"You killed two people," Jens said, "and you tried to shoot my dog."

"I could never hurt an animal." Angela's dark eyes pleaded with him.

"Give me the shotgun, Angela."

She steadied her aim. "You don't understand. I remember now, and I can't hide from myself anymore. I loved Erik, he was a good man, and I killed him. I can't live with that. So either kill me or I'll kill both of us."

"I want to understand," Jens said, stalling for time. "Tell me what happened."

For a moment, Jens thought she hadn't heard him. Then she began to speak with breathless speed, as if the words were exploding inside her.

I'd never doubted Erik," she said, "not ever. When I found that love note Marta had written him, it was like the sun had turned black, I couldn't believe how stupid I'd been. Then Licorice died, my sweet little poodle. The vet said he'd eaten poison, and I blamed myself for not keeping him safe. I fell apart, couldn't eat or sleep.

"One day, Marta came right to my front door while Erik was at work. She said horrible things—that Erik was sick of me, that he poisoned my Licorice and was going to poison me, too, so he wouldn't have to pay alimony. I felt like I was on fire. When she turned around to leave, I jumped on her back and squeezed my arm around her neck as hard as I could."

The shotgun had lowered a notch, but Jens didn't move. He might not get another chance to hear her story.

"I never thought I could kill," Angela said. "But that's what I did. Afterwards I felt cold, empty. I left Marta on a rug in Erik's study. When he came home and knelt over her body, I shot him in the back."

Jens could piece together the rest. He raised his revolver.

Angela tossed the shotgun back into the cabin and took a pistol from her pocket. She pointed it at her right temple, her finger on the trigger. "Erik didn't die right away," she said. "He called out my name. I held him in my arms, and he told me he'd just broken off the affair with Marta. He said she was evil, that I was good and gentle and he loved me."

The implications of Erik's dying statement whacked Jens upside the head. "Angela, was it Marta who killed your dog?"

"Yes." It was more a cry than a word.

Trusting his instincts, Jens lowered his revolver. "I know right now you don't want to live," he said, "but that isn't the answer. Tell me everything you have kept inside."

Angela Androwski held the pistol close to her chest, as if cuddling a puppy, and said, "You are a kind man. I want you to understand. You see, Marta wanted Erik to divorce me and marry her. At first, when he was under her spell, he agreed and started making plans. Then Marta told him to kill me so he wouldn't be burdened with alimony. She told him she'd poisoned Licorice to show him how easy it was. Erik was horrified and broke off with her. He was going to tell me everything, beg for my forgiveness. My forgiveness.

"I wanted to call 911, but Erik said he couldn't bear to think of me in jail for the rest of my life. He told me about this cabin and the false name he used when he bought it. He told me how to access his offshore accounts. Then he made me promise to get rid of…of the evidence and hide here, pretending to be him. May god have mercy on my soul, I did as he asked."

With a small sob, Angela closed her eyes and raised the pistol to her temple. Jens lunged for her arm. She staggered sideways, and with relief Jens heard the pistol land on the floor without firing. Angela lost her balance and fell backwards. Taking no chances, Jens kicked the pistol out of reach before rolling Angela on her stomach. As he was pulling her arms behind her back, Jens heard a crunching sound behind him. Angela was struggling, so he couldn't twist his head around.

"Hate to interrupt, but does this happen to belong to you?" asked a familiar voice. Ben appeared at his side, leading Mutt by his leash. "I've got handcuffs," he added. "We'd better tie the feet, too. He's still got a lot of fight in him."

"Her," Jens said.

"Well, I'll be damned," Ben said, as he saw Angela's face. "You're right, that's Angela Androwski. What the hell's going on here?"

Once they had carried Angela into the cabin and tied her to a chair, Jens sank back against the kitchen counter, and said, "I can take you to Erik and Marta's graves." He explained how he'd found them, adding, "I figured that shoe wasn't Angela's. Klara always said, 'You can tell the Other Woman by her red satin heels.'"

"Klara was a wise woman," Ben said.

"That she was." Jens glanced at their prisoner, whose head hung forward as if she'd fallen asleep.

"What made you think the killer wasn't Erik? He could have murdered both women." Ben asked.

"I considered that," Jens said. "Charity work aside, I read Erik as a hard-headed businessman. He'd need to be to be so successful. I could imagine him killing his wife to keep his money, then killing his mistress in a rage if she'd dropped him—but holing up alone in a cabin to slowly unravel? Erik might have been capable of remorse, but he'd nurse it sipping a pina colada in some country without extradition, living on his offshore savings.

"That left the gentle wife. Her gentleness is what sealed her fate," Jens said. "Angela had killed twice, both times in error, then went to live in isolation as her husband. She invented a story to ease her guilt, tried to live it every moment, but even in her story she was the villain. She couldn't escape her own conscience."

Police sirens wailed in the distance.

"The cavalry, I assume?" Jens asked.

"You betcha. Once I called the precinct and got your message to step on it, I set things in motion. You sure you don't want to come back to the Cities and work for us again?"

Jens laughed. "Not a chance," he said. "I love it up here. It's nice and quiet, especially this time of year. Nothing ever happens."

Barbara DaCosta

Barbara DaCosta is a Minneapolis-based writer with roots in Duluth who is at work on her first mystery novel. She wrote this debut story on a 1935 Underwood typewriter.

Cabin 6

Barbara DaCosta

Every time I came to Craggy Cliff Cabins, the lady at the desk said the same thing: don't go down the path beyond the cabins. The path started at the far end of the gravel road that ran past the cabins. In the late afternoon each day, whether I'd come on my own or with a boyfriend, I'd take a walk by myself to the end of the road and gaze into the often-misty green depths of the path. It led into the dense pine and birch woods that filled this secluded spit of land on the north shore of Lake Superior.

But this time, I hadn't listened to the lady. Within just a few strides, I was in the woods, the crash of the waves and the cries of the gulls suddenly muffled. I plunged forward, lungs filling with the fullness of the cool, damp, fresh air. After a few twists and turns of the path, all signs of civilization were gone.

I went around one more bend in the path, and stopped. In front of me lay a body.

It was a man, limbs tangled together as if he'd been rolled there. Locks of his shaggy, dark-blond hair were equally tangled, a patch of it matted with blood. In a contagious sort of reaction, I reached up and ran my fingers through my own hair.

The man wore standard North Woods attire. Blue jeans naturally worn out from heavy use—not artificially "stressed" on a factory assembly line. A hand-tooled leather belt, red flannel shirt over a navy T-shirt. On his feet, a hefty pair of work boots caked with mud.

From the way he looked, he was a local. An out-of-towner would have been dressed in yuppie safari-type clothes from L.L. Bean or some such upscale outfitter. An out-of-towner would be wearing a fancy multi-function watch—not the cheap Timex that this man sported.

I looked down at the man. His unnervingly open blue eyes stared up at the tops of the pine trees and the equally blue late-afternoon sky.

No wedding ring on his finger. But what did that mean? I didn't have one anymore, either. Paul and I had exchanged rings, a sign of commitment, two years ago. But those had just been re-exchanged when Paul, without a word, handed me my house key. Two years of high romance and all I got in the end was my key given back.

I looked down at the body on the ground, wondering if it was true what they say, that most murders are crimes of passion. God only knows the depths of anger I'd felt toward Paul. It didn't take much to imagine....

I shook my head to clear it. I was sleep-deprived and needed to keep focused.

What should I do now? I chewed on my fingernail. If I went to report this to the owner, I would have to confess to breaking her rules. Maybe she'd kick me out.

I hated dealing with this woman. I'd been coming to Craggy Cliff Cabins for the last five years, staying in Cabin 6 each time. The housekeeping cabins were quaint and pine-paneled. Each cabin had two bedrooms, a small bath, a fold-out couch, rocking chair, quilts, and a kitchenette outfitted with mismatched plates and cups and frying pans and pots. Several spiral-bound notebooks were stacked on a bookshelf, filled with city-dwellers' gushy entries of appreciation, pride of weekend ownership, and the occasional painful confession.

The owner was consistently distant and in a foul mood every time I'd been here; our interactions were always minimal. I'd pay up when I arrived, and slip the key—fastened to a worn, numbered, wooden disk—through the mail slot when I left. Her husband was never visible. Sometimes, when I check in, I could hear him in the other room alternately cheering and cussing at the football game on the television set, leaving her with the paperwork, the cleaning, and the clientele. Just her and her bad mood and us. Out of frustration one year, nursing my own bad temper after a bitter breakup, I'd scribbled anonymously in the current Cabin 6 notebook, "Better to call this place Crabby Cliff."

I took a deep breath. Big black flies buzzed around the body and then flew toward me. I reeled back and desperately swatted at them, just as I had reeled away from Paul when he tried to hug me after returning the key to me. A hug of guilt-offering.

A twig snapped. My head jerked up just in time to see a large buck leap away through the brush. Tears came to my eyes for a moment, but I shook my head. I had to stay focused.

The sun disappeared, and with a sudden gust, it began raining. I started back to my cabin to get my raincoat.

The purple flowers and green leaves of the lilacs shone brightly in the rain. They were blooming next to our cabin—my cabin. Paul was out of my life. I had to learn to live with that. I went in and grabbed my raincoat from among the outerwear that hung on the pegs just inside the door and walked through the bracing rain over to the office.

I rang the bell on the counter. The large, blue-printed Lake Superior circle route flyers were in a neat stack. A birchbark basket held a collection of polished agates gathered from the lakeshore; they glowed with the rich color of the iron that permeated the soil and rocks and water of northern Minnesota. On the wall hung a rosemaled wooden sign that read "Velkommen." A rack of 25¢ postcards showed the lake in all seasons: mammoth ice chunks that mimicked the shoreline cliffs, close-ups of spring wildflowers, summer upland meadows with tawny deer, bright fall colors of trees, lake, and lichens.

"Yes?" Today the owner wore a cardigan with a reindeer pattern, suitable for this inclement weather. Her blond hair was bobbed tightly to her head. The television was off, an indication that her husband was not around.

"Um, may I use your phone? It's an emergency."

She stared at me. Without a word, she picked up the phone and placed it on the counter.

I reached out for it. "I have to call the police," I explained.

"Should I dial 911, or is there a different number?"

A fleeting, tense look passed over her face.

"Just dial 911," she replied, turning toward her desk.

As I explained the situation to the sheriff's office, I could see the owner's shoulders tense up while she pretended not to eavesdrop.

When I hung up, I quickly said, "You told me not to go back there. I apologize. I'll leave right away, if you'd like."

"No need," she said stiffly, brow furrowed, crisply shuffling some file folders on her desktop.

I went to my cabin. Nothing to do but wait and wonder.

About ten minutes later, a sheriff's deputy drove up in an SUV. The rain had tapered off, and the sun was beginning to shine again.

We walked back down the path into the woods where the body lay, the wet grass staining our pants legs.

"Geez," the deputy said, looking down at the man. Some of the mud and blood had been washed off the body in the downpour.

"Do you know him?" I asked.

"Nope. Never seen him before. But that's what I'm supposed to ask you."

"Me neither." I waved another fly away. "I thought he might be someone local, given the way he's dressed."

"Yup. Sure looks that way, doesn't it?" said the deputy. He took out a small camera and snapped some pictures.

"Do you know the owners?" I asked.

"Not really. I moved up here from Duluth just last year for this job. Still don't know everyone."

"I haven't seen the cabin owner's husband," I mused. "I wonder—and there was this young couple in Cabin 5 having a big argument last night...."

"Well, we'll figure it out soon enough. So, you come up here often, then?"

"Once a year for the past five years."

"Nice place, eh?"

"Very." The deputy didn't need to know the details of my love life, how I would first take a new boyfriend on a "test drive" to Pinetree Cabins, before I'd ever dream of bringing him here to Craggy Cliff. Pinetree was another half hour up the shore and featured rickety cabins with leaky roofs and rooms that had last been painted in the 1940s.

Craggy Cliff was my real getaway, my hideaway, to be shared only with the most intimate. It was to Craggy Cliff that I also came alone to mend from broken hearts and broken promises, and it was here I'd finally brought Paul, after he grew tired of being with me at Pinetree, hearing me talk incessantly about how wonderful Craggy Cliff was.

Yes, this was a special place. I liked the isolation here. Just the waves to soothe me to sleep at night. Soothing. That's what I needed. Calm days, quiet nights. Nothing except the waves, and sometimes, late at night, the low-pitched, faint throbbing of an ore boat's engine from far off on the horizon, a distant set of lights traversing the vast world of the lake from Duluth to ports unknown.

"You staying here a while longer?" He squatted down and poked at the soil with his pen, looking to be testing its moisture.

"Yes."

"Okay, then. I'll be talking to you soon." He turned back to the body, and began taking notes.

As I walked back, a sheriff's van drove by and stopped where the path began. A deputy got out and hefted a duffel bag and box from the back of the van onto the grass, followed by a collapsible gurney.

I didn't have the heart to watch any more, so I kept going until I reached the cabins. Even so, the assertive snap of the gurney being opened traveled on the pine-scented breeze.

Cabin 5 looked deserted. The young couple's car was gone. All the stuff they'd strewn around on the wooden porch was also gone: the food chest, hiking boots, windbreakers, and picnic blanket.

Glancing around and seeing no one, I stepped onto the porch to peer in the door window. The cabin was empty except for the furnishings.

"Are you looking for something?"

I froze and slowly turned. It was the owner. She had on a turquoise slicker over her sweater and she was carrying a bucket of cleaning supplies. Behind her was the silent electric cart she used in making her housekeeping rounds. In back of the driver's seat was a cargo area filled with stacks of clean towels, blankets, and sheets, and buckets of cleaning supplies.

"I was just wondering what the other cabins looked like."

"They're all the same." She pushed past me, went inside, and firmly closed the door behind her. Through the walls, I could hear the faucet go on. There was a gurgling sound as the water made its way down the drain, and a clunk of the cupboard doors as she cleaned up after the couple.

I walked over to my cabin, a scant thirty feet away. Nestled among some trees and the lilacs, other than the closeness of Cabin 5, there was plenty of privacy. A large window overlooked the lake, and on nice days, we could sit on the porch and watch the gulls.

My stomach growled. It was time for dinner. I pulled out ingredients to make a sandwich to take down to the lake. Onion rolls from the bakery in downtown Duluth, smoked herring from Knife River, and some lettuce from the supermarket in Two Harbors, all on a paper plate. Simplicity itself. I washed my hands under the kitchen faucet with the well-used bar of Ivory soap, trying to get rid of the smell on my fingers.

Balancing my food on the plate, I climbed down the embankment until I reached the purplish basalt formation that made up much of the north shore of Lake Superior. The rocks had dried out some, but pools of water remained in wave-worn depressions.

I found my favorite spot, a natural chair formed by the rocks, where I set the food while I clambered down a bit further until I was right by the water. I squatted and reached into the lake. It was ice-cold, and I swished my hands around for a moment.

Lake Superior. Fierce and embracing. Intoxicating and calming. Life and death within one slip of the foot on a wet, mossy rock next to a deep, frigid-water drop-off.

A smooth, flat stone shone beneath the surface and caught my eye. I reached in the water for it. For whatever primal reason, a visit to the lake did not feel complete without throwing some rocks into it. Whatever the lake tossed up toward shore—mostly stones and driftwood—humans felt compelled to throw back.

I cradled the stone between my thumb and first two fingers, and then threw it, sidearm, a perfect toss. The stone, glowing in the last rays of the sun, skipped lightly across the water seven times before it disappeared.

The gulls cried loudly now, having spotted my unattended sandwich. I climbed back up and took my seat in the rock chair.

Perching the paper plate on my knees, I took a bite of my sandwich and made up stories about the dead man from the woods. Perhaps he was the resort owner's husband. That type of off-stage character who succumbs at the hands of his embittered wife. Filled with repressed rage, she whacks him with a shovel, loads him into the back of her electric cart—it was big enough to carry a body, and small enough to travel a ways on the path. She drives into the woods, his body hidden under fresh towels, and she rolls him off the back end of the cart.

The gulls circled in and landed near me, eyeing my plate. I waved my hand to shoo them away.

Maybe the man was the young husband from Cabin 5. Clobbered on the head by the young wife in a fit of well-deserved passionate anger after finding out he's cheating on her, clobbered with one of the cast-iron frying pans from the cabin's kitchenette. Yes, in the middle of the night in the midst of an argument. He staggers out the door and into the woods, where he keels over. The young woman, afraid because of what she's done, flees before morning.

I felt remorse for a moment, and threw the gulls a piece of bread crust. They swooped down and squabbled over it.

Yes, maybe the man's cheating on the woman. She's livid and loses control. Woman hits man on head with frying pan, he keels over, she sees what she's done and panics. She sneaks into the laundry shed, takes out the ever-so-quiet electric car—you could never have heard it above the waves crashing last night—drags the man's body out and loads it into the cart's bed, covering it with some towels. She drives it along the quiet, sandy shoulder of the gravel road so as to avoid waking anyone up. She steers onto the forbidden path and navigates its twists and turns as far as possible, until the ground becomes too uneven. Then she rolls the body off the back of the cart. She drives back, returns the cart, and while she's in the laundry shed, sneaks a container of cleaning solution. She returns to her cabin and spends an hour scrubbing the cabin top to bottom, the smells of cleaning products lingering in the moist air and on her hands. Finally, in the last gray minutes before the sun breaks the horizon, the waves having diminished to a gurgling sound, she creeps down the damp rocks of the cliff to the lake and flings the frying pan sidearm as far out as she can into the deep, cold waters of the lake. The frying pan for a moment seems to be weightless, then it bounces once on the surface before a wave snatches it, sucking it into the lake's depths.

I was suddenly tired. I looked at Paul's watch—it was already 9:30, but still somewhat light outdoors, a typical early summer North Woods evening. I climbed back up to the cabin and went to bed.

When I woke up the next morning, it was around 5 a.m., just as the sky was changing from dark gray dawn to daytime gray overcast. A cool, misty morning.

I wrapped myself in one of Paul's L.L. Bean sweaters and sat on the porch. A solitary gull was riding the waves. Steel gray water lapping onto purplish basalt, otherwise just silence, mesmerizing silence.

By eight, I'd eaten breakfast, washed the dishes, and packed up all of the clothes, remembering the toothbrushes at the last minute. The lingering smell of smoked fish and soap on my hands reminded me to get the leftover food from the refrigerator. I loaded the car up and went back to sit on the porch.

I looked at Paul's watch again—8:05—and pulled the strap tighter around my wrist.

There was the crunch of gravel under the wheels of a slowly approaching car. I heard the car door open and then click shut. And steps coming toward me.

Then, silence. And the waves.

"Ma'am?"

I stayed still, looking out to where the horizon would have been, where on a sunny day, one could see the distant ribbon of red sandstone cliffs on the south shore of the lake, the Wisconsin side. Paul and I had often talked about going to the south shore.

Today, there was nothing but mist. Nothing but silence and mist.

"Ma'am?" he said again, gently. "You're going to have to come with me."

Michael Allan Mallory

Michael Allan Mallory grew up in Minneapolis and graduated from the University of Minnesota with a degree in English Literature. During daylight hours he works with computer and network systems in the Information Technology field. After the sun sets he delves into murkier pursuits, among them studying and teaching wing chun kung fu and practicing Chen style Tai Chi. Chief among his interests is wife Cathy, a delightful companion who is the only other human in the House of Cats, which is populated by an orange tabby who thinks he's a dog, and a purebred Maine Coon who thinks he's a rooster. They live in St. Louis Park.

Death Roll, his debut novel with Marilyn Victor, was published in May 2007 and features the first zoologist sleuth in the person of Lavender "Snake" Jones. When the director of the Minnesota Valley Zoo shows up as a late night snack in the new crocodile exhibit, Snake must use her knowledge of animal behavior to ferret out the identity of the real killer.

Michael is currently working on the second Snake Jones mystery with Marilyn, which is set in Ely and deals with the gray wolf.

Bird of Prey

Michael Allan Mallory

The next kill. She is it. That much he knew. What he didn't
know was how she would die. So far he hadn't repeated himself; the others had gone quickly, without mess, and most impor-
tantly, without a discernable M.O. All dead-end cases.

The Falcon took a long drink from his coffee cup, watching
the young woman three tables in front of him. Cindy, that was
her name. Cindy Fawcett. Her blonde hair shimmered to her
shoulders like in the shampoo commercials, and she sat like a
woman schooled in good posture and proper table manners.
He'd been studying her every move since he first set eyes on
her, watching what she did and how she did it. For three days
in a row it was the same breakfast: Cheerios with skim milk, a
peach yogurt and a small orange juice. He'd learned all he could
about her habits, like how she went for an extended hike into the
forest every day after lunch. He'd even followed her once—at a
distance.

Now, as then, she was completely unaware of him. Nondescript
they called it. That used to annoy him, being thought of as wallpaper.
But now he understood it was his advantage; being unmemorable
was as close to being invisible as you could get. The Falcon smiled
into his coffee. Like the predator whose name he took, he envisioned
himself soaring high above his prey, targeting them while they were
oblivious to his presence. Then, tucking in his wings, he dropped
out of the sky and onto them like a thunderbolt. Yeah, that was him,
an unstoppable killing force—

"Hi! You look lonely here all by yourself," chirped a jarringly
happy voice. "Mind if I join you?"

Startled, the Falcon looked up to see a chunky middle-aged woman with a cheerful round face slide into the chair opposite him.

Damn. She blocked his view of Cindy.

"Actually, I—"

"My name is Mary Jane Bauman," she sang with far more energy than he cared to hear this early in the morning. "I'm in Cabin One." She looked at him expectantly.

"Um, the name is Darrell. Darrell Johnson." The name he used to make the reservations.

"What cabin are you in, Darrell?"

"Number ten."

"Nice! I hear it's got a terrific view of the harbor." Mary Jane dug into her breakfast with enthusiasm, shoveling forkfuls of scrambled eggs into her mouth. If he were lucky maybe she'd choke on them, he thought.

"It's okay," he said with disinterest, trying to sound boring in hopes she'd move on to another table.

"First time at Eagle's Nest?"

"Yeah."

"Me too! Isn't Lake Kabetogama gorgeous? I wish I could go on the water but I burn so easily. And you wouldn't think that'd be a problem being so far north. I mean, we're practically spitting distance to Canada. But it's still a hot one out there."

Get up. That's all you have to do. Just get up, and walk away from this annoying woman! The Falcon moved his legs beneath him, ready to push himself away from the table when he stopped with a realization—maybe this worked for him. Cindy had turned to look at something behind her, something pointed out by her breakfast companions. She was looking right past him. If she noticed him at all right now it would be with this Mary Jane woman; perhaps Cindy would think they were together, looking like so many other vacationing couples eating breakfast at the old spruce lodge. Which meant that later, when he approached her alone, she might let her guard down. Yeah, that might work. And it was only for breakfast. He could stand Mary Jane Big Ass for a little while longer. After all, keeping his cool was how he'd gotten away with the other killings.

"It's so beautiful here," said Mary Jane. "So peaceful and remote."

Remote, yes. Voyageurs National Park's dense conifer forest offered endless prospects for dumping a body. The Falcon stole another look at Cindy, who joked with the older married couple at her table.

"Are you from the Cities, Darrell?"

"No, Des Moines." Which was a lie. He didn't need her to know he was from Minneapolis.

"Up here by yourself?" She inspected his left hand.

"Yeah."

"Me too!" she laughed. Although he didn't know what the hell was so damned funny. "What do you do in Des Moines?"

"I'm a plumber."

"That must be interesting work."

Really? What's so frickin' interesting about cleaning out other people's toilets? In point of fact, he worked at a sanitary landfill, which was still mucking through other people's crap. He offered Mary Jane a brittle smile, darting a quick look at Cindy, who was turned in profile. Goddamn, she's good lookin'! Playmate material. Maybe this one deserved special attention before he snuffed out her lights, a little extra hands-on action.

The Falcon grunted with amusement.

"—Yes," clucked Mary Jane between mammoth bites of blueberry pancakes, "I thought it was funny, too."

He had no idea what the woman was talking about. He had tuned her out a minute ago. God, the woman never stopped yammering! Stick a sock in it, why don't you? But he couldn't say that. Creating a scene would attract attention, attention he didn't want, especially in a place as public as the breakfast room. Too many people to remember him. And being remembered could land him in prison. For that reason, he sucked it up and did a slow, silent, burning count to ten.

"You married, Darrell?"

"Uh, no."

"Me neither."

Why did he tell her that? Now she'd be all over him. Okay, okay, you can fix this.

"Actually, I'm going through a break up," he offered in a hangdog manner. "My divorce was finalized two weeks ago. That's part of the reason I'm up here. Like you said, to get away. Sorry, I'm not in a mood to talk; the whole divorce thing's got me bummin'."

"You poor dear!" Mary Jane buttered her wheat toast and tossed him sympathy. "I just figured you weren't a morning person. I'm sorry if I touched a tender spot." She then prattled on how her sister, Regina, was also going through a divorce, looking at him with a little too much interest.

A movement to the side caught his attention. Cindy was up and moving to the trash bin. Bussing her tray, the young woman turned to go, unaware that a piece of cloth had fallen from the back pocket of her form-hugging shorts.

Perfect! The Falcon shoved back his chair. "Sorry, I have to go." He left Mary Jane Bauman blinking in his wake. He put away his breakfast dishes, then bent down to retrieve the lost article: a terry-cloth headband. Snatching it up, he savored the feel of the material between his fingertips.

"Excuse me, Miss." He ran up to Cindy, who had exited the lodge in the direction of the paddleboats. "You dropped this."

"Oh. Thank you." The pretty blonde smiled back. "That was nice of you." Cindy Fawcett couldn't have been older than twenty-seven, he figured, her youthfulness reflected in her friendly, bouncy manner. So trusting.

"Are you a runner?" He indicated the headband.

"More of a power walker, I guess."

"Ah," the Falcon feigned recognition, "I think I've seen you on one of the trails. Not the bog walk, it was in the forest."

"Yup; it was probably me. I love being in the deep woods, love listening to the birds, particularly when you've got them all to yourself. It's…so soothing. Don't you think?"

The Falcon smiled a thin, predatory smile. "Yes, exactly." Be charming. You can be charming. Get her guard down. "I'm Darrell, by the way." He offered his hand. She accepted it. Hers was small, soft and surprisingly warm.

"Cindy," she beamed with tantalizing sexuality.

It was wrong to smile like that if she didn't mean it.

"Are you here for the whole week?" he asked.

"No, I'm leaving Saturday. Got to get back to the job. You know how it is. And you?"

"I'm heading out Friday. Promised my sister I'd help her move."

"Oh, how sweet."

Fell for that one, too. He was making good progress, just enough to get closer to her next time— Stop. Don't think about it. Don't give off any bad vibes or you'll creep her out. Be cool.... "Well, Cindy, it was nice to meet you. I should let you get on your way."

Good, she's still smiling at you.

He waved goodbye and strolled along the beach satisfied his plan was coming together. She trusted him a little now, enough to let him get closer next time without raising suspicion. And he'd learned when she was checking out. Three days to Saturday. Two days left for Cindy Fawcett to live.

★ ★ ★

Concealed among a stand of tamaracks and jack pines, the Falcon scanned for movement on the trail, most of which was obscured from his view by thick underbrush. Glimpses of the winding path appeared to him between pine-needled branches, and he took comfort in the fact that it would be just as difficult to see him, even more so being dressed in drab olive green.

He checked his watch. Sixty-two minutes. That's how long ago Cindy had passed by. If she stuck to her usual after lunch timetable, she should be back within the next half hour. The Falcon couldn't believe his luck. Few, if any, of the other resort guests knew about this trail set within the thick woods. And many of those who tried it for the first time soon had second thoughts. The rugged path, full of steep inclines, ruts and low branches, usually compelled less ambitious hikers to give up half a mile back. Not Cindy Fawcett, who attacked the trail with the nimbleness of a boot camp Marine.

Ideal location. No witnesses. Even a waterfall fifty yards back loud enough to muffle a scream. And if Cindy took her time returning, he could wait. There was no other way back, just dense woods and bogs. It didn't get any better than this. Let her take her time; he could be patient. Very patient. Just ask Linda. Well, if she were still alive you could ask her, he mused. For her he had waited nearly two hours in the rain, soaked to the skin outside the St. Paul bistro, undeterred in his goal. When Linda fought back harder than he'd expected it inflamed him all the more. The adrenaline rush was unlike anything he'd ever known, the sense of complete mastery over her, the feeling of accomplishment. Until that night he'd been a nobody, just another forgettable loser. Not now. For on that night he had finally discovered his life's purpose. After Linda he became the Falcon.

Just thinking of the next kill sent an electric charge through his skin. Anticipating Cindy's firm young body struggling against his made him flush with excitement. Strange. It has never been about sex before. Well, she is a looker. Trouble with sex was it would leave DNA. Messy. Unless he disposed of the body so it could never be found. Glancing around, he found assurance in several ready places of concealment in the underbrush. Not fool proof but—

Snap!

The breaking twig alerted him. He spun round, his eyes sweeping the foliage for movement. Nothing. For an instant he believed a foraging squirrel was the culprit until an irritatingly familiar voice called to him through the low fir branches.

"Hi, Darrell! I thought that was you." Mary Jane Bauman stepped into view from behind a broad-skirted tamarack. "You're really off the path!" she said, breathless.

What the frickin' hell was her fat ass doing here? The stupid bitch was going to ruin everything!

His rage swelled like a storm surge; it took all he had to keep from seizing the rock at his feet and whacking it against her skull. As supremely satisfying as that might be, it had no part in his master plan. Mistakes happened when people acted on the spur of the moment and improvised themselves into trouble. Sticking to the plan was what had kept him out of danger every other time.

Steady and cool. Keep your head.

He jammed his eyes closed and hissed out a lungful of air.

"Are you okay?" asked Mary Jane. She adjusted the waistband of her plus size sweats. The black fanny pack really didn't do much for her figure. "You don't look good."

"Headache," he told her. Yeah, and you're the reason for it!

"Really? Such an odd spot to be resting—"

"I was meditating, wanted a few minutes alone."

Mary Jane pulled her fanny pack round her ample midsection, bringing the pouch to the front. Unzipping it, she rummaged. "I have some Tylenol...."

Time was slipping away. If Cindy came back now he'd miss his best chance. And he'd never get another opportunity as good as this again. Tomorrow she'd check out of the resort. If he didn't kill her now it wouldn't happen. Problem was he had to first get rid of Mary Jane—

Get rid of Mary Jane.

Ah! Maybe his first impulse had been right after all. Her head was bowed as she searched the contents of the fanny pack; she wasn't even looking at him.

Opportunity screamed: Screw the plan! When Fate hands you an opportunity on a silver platter, you don't ignore it. Seize the moment! Capitulating to necessity, he bent down in one smooth motion for the rock. One quick swing. Just one—

"Don't move, Darrell."

The cold authority of her voice made him look up and into the muzzle of a 9 mm automatic pistol. His eyes flicked up to the woman behind it, who regarded him with the keen interest of a scientist monitoring a lab rat. "Back up, please." She jerked the pistol toward him; its black muzzle hungering for a bite of his abdomen.

"What the—?"

"Just a few more steps, Darrell. I want you a little more out of sight. Good. Right there."

"Put that gun down bef—"

Crack! Crack!

Two reports erupted from the muzzle in rapid succession. Bewildered, he stared back. She shot me! The bitch shot me! He clutched his abdomen and sank to his knees, glaring at her through the pain in search of an explanation. Instead of getting one, he was met with a digital camera trained on his every action. She was making a damn video!

"Does it hurt bad, Darrell? Talk to me. How's it feel?"

He collapsed to the ground, grimacing from fire raging in his gut.

"Fabulous!" She zoomed in for a close up. "I want to know everything you feel. That's why I'm recording it. See, I'm a writer. I'm doing research for my next book. You probably haven't read my first series. They're cozies. My sleuth runs a shoe boutique in a suburban mall. I did okay with them but my agent wanted me to do something with a harder edge. The critics said I was too much Mrs. Suburban Housewife to tackle anything more menacing. Well, I showed them!"

The feeling had left the Falcon's legs. He could barely focus on her through the pain; breathing was difficult, like sucking air through a Barcalounger.

"I'm on the third book of my new series," Mary Jane announced with pride. "It's very dark. Graphic violence. Stuff Ginny O'Keefe would never handle. Ginny is my character from the shoe boutique series. It's like I'm channeling a totally different writer. All these evil, twisted thoughts come pouring out of me. The thing is I didn't have experience with actual murders, so I decided to research each murder in detail." She held up the camera.

Shut up. Just shut up! The voice in his head screamed yet only a broken gurgle escaped his throat.

Mary Jane crouched for a different angle. "This is great. I hope it doesn't hurt too much, Darrell. See, for each book I choose a different murder method. I poisoned the first victim. The second I ran down with a rider mower. Man, that was messy, so for the new book I thought I'd go for something quick and neat—a shooting." She flashed him a nervous smile. "I'm really sorry I had to kill you. But yesterday you sounded so depressed, I figured it was a win–win situation. I end your suffering and I get the realistic details I need."

Darkness smothered the Falcon's consciousness in a slow, fatal embrace. The last thing he heard, as if rising from the depths of a bottomless grotto, was the voice of Mary Jane Bauman.

"Funny how most people don't know it's me writing the new series. I use a pen name—Kestrel Larkin. Like it? What's crazy is I've actually recycled some of my old plots. Changed a few things around. Nobody notices! The big difference is the narrative voice; it's sassy and tough. The main thing I've learned from this experience is that it's not the idea that really matters, Darrell, it's the execution."

Moira F. Harris

Moira Harris is an art historian and the author of Museum of the Streets: Minnesota's Contemporary Outdoor Murals. *She has also written about other aspects of popular culture, including the St. Paul Winter Carnival, the Hamm's beer bear, painted Sicilian donkey carts, and poker-playing dogs. Her most recent publication is* Minnesota On Paper: Collecting Our Printed History *(University of Minnesota Press).*

She and her husband Leo are the proprietors of Pogo Press.

The Body at Dust Bowl Lake

Moira F. Harris

Everybody saw him. Everybody, the reporter learned, even the people who were too young to see anything or were out of town that day. It was very much a case of "his say," "her say," and "their say." Their say, the reporter always thought, meant when you'd heard a story so often that you thought it had happened to you. Sometimes there was a lot of their say you had to sift through.

There were a lot of strange things about what should have been a simple story. He'd been a brand new reporter then, new to the paper, new to his job, and new to reporting anywhere for anybody. So it was his first story and he wanted to do it right even if it seemed filler stuff, not exactly breaking news, and certainly not something that, as it turned out, would have legs, long legs.

His editor wanted him to go out to one of the Swedish towns, interview a few of the older folks, and come back with something about what it had been like when the lakes dried up in the thirties. "Get 'em to tell you about Minnesota in Dust Bowl days," he'd said.

At first everybody told him just about the same thing. It had been hard. People lost their jobs and their savings. The banks closed. Tourists didn't come and fishermen stayed away. That was the story his editor expected, but he found something else. It was a hidden story, a real mystery. He always tried to remember what he'd asked that led him to the story. He certainly didn't say, casually, "Have there been any murders here?" But one of his questions opened hidden drawers of memories and once they were open what remained of the story was there for the writing.

He could have begun by writing that a stranger had come to town, but he hadn't, and that was lucky because it would not have been true although he didn't know it then. He'd started the story with what he did know for sure and that was that everyone up town that day had seen the man. He had arrived on one of the midmorning trains, not the earliest one because that was filled with fishermen, but a later one. He stepped out of the coach and when he walked through the depot people noticed because he was so well, so properly dressed for summer. Blue jacket, white pants, black and white shoes, Panama hat. Almost too well dressed, some said, but they liked the idea that he'd come in those clothes to stay at the hotel. Showed good manners, they said. He carried a suitcase, but it was quite small, worn, and a bit shabby. Not as nice as the clothes.

Then he walked out of the depot. That was the first strange thing. The jitney was there at the depot waiting to pick up all the guests and drive them to the hotel, but he didn't get in. It was as if he knew exactly where he was going, but he didn't want to get there yet.

Central saw him from the telephone office in the park (where it was then). She remembered that he walked through the park to the post office. Usually people who came to the hotel would go to the post only after they'd been at the hotel a few days. They'd buy their postcards, write "Wish you were here," mail them and then get home before the postcards reached their neighbors. Central thought he must have had some very important letter to send.

The farmers driving their wagons full of milk cans to the creamery saw him. The wagon line was long that morning, stretching through town, as it was still early in the day. The farmers noticed him because he'd waited on the high sidewalk in front of the new bank until every one of the wagons went past. Very polite, some of them said. Usually city folks just pushed their way through the line making the horses stop short as if city folks were important and wagons of milk weren't. But he waited, so they saw him. At least some of them recollected that he'd headed over to the drugstore. The druggist said the man had come in and asked to buy a blue toothbrush. The druggist had suggested other colors, but he said it had to be blue, like his jacket. The druggist offered to phone the Cities, but it was Saturday, after all, and he was fresh out and there couldn't possibly be any more anything until Monday so he was sorry. The man said he was sorry, too.

The kids saw him. On a weekend there were usually at least some kids waiting for the trains. Boys wanted to put pennies on the rails so the train would squash them. Girls didn't go there as often, just when there was somebody to meet. One girl, he'd heard, even got into a fight about going to the station. She was all dressed up, ready to meet her father who was coming for the weekend from Duluth. A neighbor boy teased her, she slugged him with a Sir Walter Raleigh tobacco can, and they had to go to the doctor to get his forehead stitched up. That is, her mother, his mother, and the boy went. The girl stayed home and didn't go to the station after all and she remembered that all her life.

Since so many people said that they had seen the man, the reporter asked what the man looked like. One woman said, "Not too tall, but slender like Fred Astaire, and he walked on the balls of his feet." The reporter wanted to follow up by asking if he danced down Main Street, but decided not to. Another woman said, "No, he was tall like Gary Cooper and took long strides as if he was crossing the prairies after something." The reporter tried to learn if the man had been handsome or ugly, young or old (after he'd given up on thin or fat and tall or short), but most people settled on "medium" or "average" as a description. The problem seemed to be that no one had really looked at his face (staring wasn't really polite) so they couldn't say what color his eyes were, or the shade of his hair or the size of his nose. But they did recall his clothes, and on that they all agreed: blue jacket, white pants, black and white shoes, Panama hat.

But to return to the man. Next he headed across the street to the sidewalk in front of the barbershop. There he took out his watch. Some people said it was a gold watch on a long chain. Some people said it was just a shiny pocket watch, but everybody agreed that he looked at it as if he hadn't been able to check the time in the drugstore or look in the barbershop window at their big new clock. The barber thought the man's haircut was old, out of fashion, a little too long on the sides and back. That was what he remembered. The men in the garage saw him, but he didn't seem unusual to them.

The man kept on walking, not too fast, not too slow, past the chapel. There were plenty of people in the chapel that day getting ready for Mavis's shower. It was to be a luncheon so they still had tables to set, flowers to put out, and a place to arrange for presents. Mavis was very popular so there were sure to be lots of gifts. Most of the church ladies were so busy indoors that they didn't see the man passing by on the sidewalk.

So he walked on, not really unnoticed, but unremembered, past the neat white houses with the generous porches, past the tidy gardens full of roses and peonies, dancing or striding (the accounts did vary) on the sidewalk that went only along the west side of the street. Then he reached the hotel, passed between its brick pillars, and entered the lobby presided over by the musty figure of a stuffed loon.

He'd booked a single room so there was no trouble checking in, especially when he paid in advance, in cash. When they looked on the register later, he'd written his name and address clearly. The constable asked Central to check the address in the phone books for the Cities, but no one was surprised to hear that there was no such street, no such place. He'd come from town on the train, but that was all most people would know about him, ever.

He said he really wasn't hungry for lunch; he thought he'd just rest a bit. Later in the afternoon he walked around the grounds, looked at the rock gardens, and watched the other guests play tennis. He'd said no to golf, or canoeing, walked right past the slot machines (which weren't supposed to be there), but he did try bowling. Would you believe that he rolled a perfect game even though everyone thought he'd slide right off the alley in those slippery shoes? Not many guests did that.

Verna served him dinner in the big dining room and she said there had been nothing odd about that. He sat by himself at one of their nicer tables with a good view of the lake. He'd ordered the regular menu, eaten everything ("a real plate polisher"), and just had water to drink. She'd asked if he wanted anything stronger, or even coffee, but he'd said no, very politely. Since Verna seemed to have talked to him the most, people wanted to know if he sounded foreign, but she didn't think so. Whenever she was asked, she'd answer, "He talked just like you and me. Could have come from around here." And then everybody would shake his or her head in amazement.

After dinner almost all the guests went out to the pavilion and either danced or just listened to the band. It really had been a lovely night. Clear sky, stars, birds calling across what was left of the water. Even a loon called, announcing its territory. Most people were certain that he hadn't stayed behind in the pavilion. He'd walked slowly, thoughtfully (somebody said, although that was a later guess), back along the boardwalk to the hotel. Then everyone went to bed and the lights went off, one by one, in the hotel and the cottages.

The next morning the beach crew found the body when they went to get the boats and canoes ready. He was lying there, partly in the water, dressed in the same blue jacket and white pants they'd seen him wear the day before. First people wondered if he'd slipped off the boardwalk and fallen in the water, but surely he would have screamed for help and people were carrying flashlights so they would have seen him or been able to find him.

No, somehow he must have fallen, or even been killed. Killed, that was an awful thought. Had Dillinger, or Capone, or Karpis suddenly come and finished him off, rubbed him out, or equaled the score or whatever people like that did? Everybody knew that there had been gangsters living in Bald Eagle and White Bear. Maybe they'd come farther north to hide out and they'd seen him. He hadn't looked like a gangster, but maybe he was and they just hadn't noticed. A gangster without a toothbrush. Some people couldn't get over that.

The hotel manager told his crew to remove the body immediately. It was bad for business to leave it on the beach, but the only place anyone could think to put it was in the icehouse. It wasn't a truly hot day, but still ice would preserve the body until the coroner had a look. So they carried him, leaving a dripping trail of water and seaweed that had to be cleaned up quickly (bad for business), to the icehouse. There they spread him out as carefully as possible on top of the sawdust and the ice. They straightened his clothes, put his hat on his head (the hat had floated out a bit in the lake, but they still managed to save it), and made it almost seem as if they were burying him there in the ice like those bodies in the Alps that people find.

Then they called Sven the constable who walked over (he never did have a car), followed by a smallish group of people who wondered what could be wrong at the hotel. Sven declared that the man was certainly dead, he didn't know him, and he would call the sheriff. It was Sunday by now, and the sheriff's wife had planned a picnic with her relatives after church. He wasn't looking forward to it, but he always said no first, and her family came over anyway. He said NO this time, very firmly, on account of police business, and drove all the way over to the hotel. There wasn't much he could do, except agree that he didn't know the man either. Since the man was definitely dead, and perfectly safe in the icehouse, they could wait until the next day to have the coroner do his work.

So the sheriff drove home. The case was strange, but under control. When he parked in the driveway his wife was just setting out the gelatin salads on the picnic tables. Cherry again, he said to himself. Always cherry. Today it made him think of the blood that wasn't there. He hadn't seen any bullet holes, or gaping wounds, or bumps of any kind on the man's head, but the coroner could figure out how he died.

It was about midnight, more or less, people said, when they saw the flames shooting up. They thought at first the hotel was burning again, but it was fine and so were the cottages, the boathouse, the beer garden. and the separate bathrooms (for men and women). The icehouse was on fire and before the fire department could assemble their equipment the icehouse burned to the ground. There was nothing left to save. It always seemed strange that an icehouse could burn, but it did. What was even more peculiar was the body. Everyone was guessing that it would be scarred or scorched, but it wasn't. In fact there was no body in the ruins of the icehouse. It was gone. Why would someone take the body and burn the icehouse? What was the connection of the man to the hotel or to the town? Now the sheriff and the constable had two crimes, two mysteries, to solve, and as the reporter wrote, they never were able to solve either one.

The coroner, when they called him, was put out. He'd investigated plenty of accidents, but never a murder, if this had been one. He'd even rearranged his whole schedule on Monday so he could do a thorough job. He had planned time to write up his findings and complete the paperwork. Now there was no body, no murder, no wrongful death, and no case. In fact, the sheriff had announced that the case was closed. It was over and done with. He and the constable would try to determine the cause of the fire, but the coroner was not needed. The coroner thought sadly about the missed opportunity and excitement as he returned to his regular routine.

The reporter finished his story, took the train back to town, and turned in what he'd written. His editor offered tepid praise as after all there was no conclusion, but he liked what there was well enough to run it on the page with local oddities, like huge misshapen potatoes or one-legged mountain climbers who've reached the top of Mt. Everest.

For the reporter it was the beginning. He went on to write other crime stories. He worked in Chicago, in Philadelphia, and finally New York before retiring. Every once in a while he would think about his first story that still seemed incomplete. Perhaps, now that he was retired, he could take the time to go back to Minnesota, check up on old buddies, maybe fish a bit, and even visit Dust Bowl Lake.

When he stopped by the newsroom in St. Paul there weren't many familiar faces. The reporters and editors he'd known had moved on, retired, or died. The road north was new to him, too. He could have taken the freeway, but decided to drive the old road and check the changes from the past.

In the town nearest to Dust Bowl Lake he was flattered to find that people in the local newspaper office had heard of him.

His old story was even in a frame on the wall, but to everyone there it remained a mystery, a very cold case. One kid (was he really out of high school, the reporter wondered) said that whenever anyone had questions about the past, they interviewed the historian.

"The historian?" repeated the reporter. Why hadn't he found the historian? And exactly who was he? The answer came that he was neither a teacher nor a writer, but was someone who'd been born in the town, grown up there, then moved away for a while, then come back to live with his daughter.

"He's really, really old," continued the kid, "but he knows more about things that have happened here than anyone else ever will. We can call his daughter and see if he'd be willing to talk to you."

It took only ten minutes to drive over to a small white house hidden behind huge evergreens at the south end of Dust Bowl Lake. The historian's daughter met him at the door and showed him into the parlor where her father sat.

"Dad," she said, "this is the reporter the newspaper people called about. He wants to hear stories about when the lake was dry."

Her father nodded a welcome, pointed to the chair next to his, and the reporter sat down. The daughter had warned him to speak slowly and clearly, and to look straight at her father. But before he could ask anything, he realized that the historian was waiting. When the screen door slammed shut, the historian relaxed, and asked what the reporter wanted to know.

The reporter mentioned the body at Dust Bowl Lake, the body that had disappeared, and the historian sighed for a moment. Then he said yes, he did know something about that. But first would the reporter please put away his notebook.

"I've kept this secret all these years," the historian said, "and I don't intend to break my promise now."

The reporter thought for a moment about "the people's right to know" and then decided it wasn't so important. He'd much rather hear the story now, than write it.

The historian began by saying that the dead man had grown up in town; he had been a neighbor in fact, living in the older part of the city. His family was poor and he was the only child. He hadn't finished school, partly because there was no high school in town then, but mostly because his folks had died and he'd gone off to the war, the Great War. He'd been a sort of hero, but after the war he didn't come back.

"Didn't your papers write about the War, the casualties and the survivors?" the reporter asked.

"Oh yes," said the historian. "There was even a fancy book with gold print on the cover published afterwards. Every soldier who went from the county was in the book, except my neighbor. I did ask the editor about that and he said there'd been a mistake. I was right. He should have been listed. They'd left him out partly because they'd forgotten he came from here and then they couldn't find a photograph so that was that.

"He was an outsider," the man from Dust Bowl Lake continued. "A Finlander in a town of Swedes so maybe he didn't feel welcome any more." The historian didn't know whether that was really the case. Why Finns, like the man's parents, had come there he didn't know either, but probably it was because of the mill and the logging.

Anyway, like everyone else, he'd totally forgotten about the man who had been his neighbor until he received the letter. It said, partly, that the man had come back home to die. He had no family, no kin, and no money. The jacket and pants he wore were all he owned. So "if something happened to me" would his neighbor, out of long ago friendship, see that his body received a proper burial? There could not be a church service if the man took his own life, but a burial there should be.

That long ago Sunday morning, when the reporter's new source heard about the death from Central (who could be astoundingly helpful at times in spreading the news), he knew what he had to do. If he removed the body, buried it, and burned the icehouse (leaving no clues or traces to follow), his duty would be quietly and completely done. So he did just that. The historian felt sorry that he had never put a marker on the grave. Then he decided that perhaps his friend had not expected that.

"Where did you bury the body?" the reporter asked.

"Well," said the Minnesota man, "do you know those Indian

mounds that are all over the place? We used to have some really big ones on the bluff above our lake so I just used one of them. Someday if archaeologists decide to dig and the water hasn't covered everything up, they'll find a Finlander and his gold watch with the Chippewa. A new warrior with the old. They'll be busy for years trying to figure that out!"

The reporter had many questions about the case and most were answered. Why hadn't townspeople recognized the man? Most of them, Verna and the beach crew especially, were born long after he left town, he was told. The constable should have known whose body it was, but his eyes no longer worked too well (there'd been an accident years ago when he was lighting streetlights) so if people said something was true, and they did, then Sven would agree. It was just easier that way.

But mostly they didn't recognize the man because they hadn't expected to know him. People from the town went to the hotel for meals or meetings, and to dance on the weekends to the music of the Cracker Jack Club band. Local people didn't spend the night in the hotel or the cottages. A local person, even one who had moved away, would have talked, maybe just a little, to somebody. So because he didn't, they saw only the clothes and were sure he was not, nor had ever been, one of them.

"Was there anything else in the letter?" the reporter asked.

"Not really," replied the historian. "Just two other words. 'I failed.' I wasn't sure how he had failed or what he had been doing, but I figured it was like some of the folks I knew back then. When people lost their money and their farms, they really felt as if it was over. They had failed and they didn't want to talk any more about it. You'd just find a body out in the fields."

The reporter hesitated, just for a moment, before he asked if his new acquaintance would tell him the man's name. But the answer, as he expected, was no. No one needed to know that, it was a long time ago now, and the man had what he wanted, a resting place by Dust Bowl Lake. He had come back home, but no one would ever need to know where.

The reporter and the historian heard the front door open, so the reporter rose, said thank you and good-bye. Then he drove back to the old road, headed north, and hoped that the fishing on that small lake he remembered would be just as fine as ever.

Judith Yates-Borger

Judith Yates-Borger's long journalistic career includes newspaper and magazine reporting and magazine editing. She has also published two works of nonfiction. Her awards include the Frank Premack Award for Public Affairs Journalism, the Strong Award for Business Writing, numerous honors from the Society for Professional Journalists, and the Associated Press Sports Editors Award for coverage of the Minnesota Gopher men's basketball scandal.

"Hunter's Lodge" is Judith's first foray into the realm of mystery fiction. She began this new tack after rioters in North Minneapolis fire-bombed her car while she was reporting for the St. Paul Pioneer Press. *She is writing her second mystery novel.*

Judith lives in Minneapolis with her husband. Their three grown children live nearby. Since 1982, the family has swum, water-skied, sunned, laughed, cried, and relaxed at Northern Pine Lodge, near Park Rapids, Minnesota.

Hunter's Lodge

Judith Yates-Borger

My family made our first trip first to Hunter's Lodge when I was three years old. Every year since, we have come at the same time—last week in July, first week in August—and stayed in the same cabin. Most of the other families do the same. For two weeks every year, it's our own little community. Everybody knows everybody.

When I was five, I fed the bunnies. At eight I was the first kid in line for hotdog and hayride night. At ten I learned to water ski. It was the place where the best memories of my youth were born.

Which is why I was upset the night we found the body.

It started out like most nights at the cabin. I was twenty-six at the time. About ten o'clock my brothers—Patrick, who is a year younger than I, and George, who is two years younger—pulled on our swimsuits and headed for the sauna. We sat there until our skin began to crisp, as ususal, and then ran off the end of the dock. The lake, which had felt like it was filled with bath water during the day, was cool and soothing at night. Once we'd cooled down we returned to the sauna, eventually running back and forth between the sauna and the lake half a dozen times. Then we built a bonfire on the beach and broke out the beer.

This night we were on about our fourth run when George grabbed my arm. I thought he was just trying to slow me down, so I pulled away and ran as fast as I could to jump in the lake.

"Katie," he said, pointing toward the shore, after following me into the water. "Look."

"It's a log," I said. "So what?"

"I don't think so. It looks like it's wearing a shirt," he replied.

"What?" asked Patrick who, as usual, had been the first one in the lake.

George pointed again and we all stared. Clouds blocked out any light the moon might have bestowed on us. Something long and thin floated back and forth in the waves lapping gently against the shore.

"It's just a toy one of the kids left in the water," Patrick said.

"I don't think so," George replied again.

I hung back while my brothers swam for shore. They had reached water shallow enough to walk when I decided to follow them. I was 10 feet from the "log," when I heard Patrick say, "Holy shit, it's a body."

The dead man wore dark pants and a white shirt. He still had on shoes.

"I thought drowned bodies were supposed to be bloated and gushy," George said. "This one isn't. It just looks like a guy floating face down."

Patrick leaned down, flipped it over and recoiled. "Guess he didn't drown."

The dead guy was white with dark brown hair and about six feet tall, with a beard. He had a knife wound just under his ribs.

"Jesus," George said. "Now what do we do?"

We woke up our parents and the owners of the resort, who called the only cop in Park Rapids, Minnesota. We could hear his police car speeding down the mile-long washboard dirt road into the lodge. That was the year Bucky, the owner, had pounded imitation eyes, noses and mouths into most of the trees, making them look like tall, lean old men. With the red and blue lights flashing against them, the trees seemed to march closer and closer to the lake. Meanwhile, the loons began to call.

All the commotion woke up the families staying in the other 20 cabins. People stood around in their pajamas with flashlights, trying to keep the kids out of the cop's way while still getting a good look themselves. What with the Park Rapids volunteer fire department, the medical examiner and who knows who else, it took almost all night to get the body out of there.

My brothers and I never got the bonfire, or the beer.

★ ★ ★

About 2 o'clock the next afternoon, I crawled out of bed and headed to the lodge for a cup of coffee and a sticky bun. The lodge, built of logs in the 1920s, is where we play cards on red and white checkered oil cloth-covered decrepit card tables. We catch up on who is married, or in jail, or got caught smoking weed in the 120 back acres of pines and ponds. There are two pool tables off to one side, and a half dozen pinball machines against the back wall. A faded poster from the Minnesota Department of Natural Resources hangs on a post, warning boaters to check their props for Eurasian milfoil.

"Thanks for babysitting yesterday," said Sally, who owns the lodge with Bucky. Sally was working behind the counter. "I know you're supposed to be on vacation but I don't know what I would have done without you."

"No problem." I climbed on a red swivel bar stool. "Joey's my favorite. I remember when he was born. It almost feels like he's my little brother. But I just couldn't keep him in his room. I hope we didn't cause any trouble when I had to come and get him out of the kitchen while you talked."

"I told Meg I'd watch the little guy, but then the developer arrived and we really needed to be able to talk without interruption."

"That guy was a developer?"

Sally nodded. "He wants to buy the resort, carve it up into plots and sell them to people who would build their own cabins."

"You're not going to sell, are you?" I was horrified at the thought.

"We don't want to, but Bucky and I are getting older and running a resort like this is getting tough," she said. "He wants to call it a 'Northwoods gated community.' Offered us $10 million."

"Don't your kids want to take over?" I asked.

"They've had enough of living at a resort," she replied.

★ ★ ★

I felt that constriction in my throat that happens when I'm furious. How could anyone even think about changing this fabulous place? It was paradise and some jerk wants to take it away from us, I thought. It just couldn't happen. My eyes started to sting, a sure sign I was going to cry. I didn't want Sally to see that so I changed the subject.

"Any news about the body?" I asked.

"I thought you knew. That was the developer," Sally said.

"You're kidding," I replied. "Really?"

"Bucky made the identification last night," Sally said.

Neither of us said anything for a long time. The only sound in the room was the soft ping of the pinball machines. Molly helped a couple of kids check out clubs for miniature golf and a couple who wanted ping pong paddles.

Done with those tasks, she returned to my spot at the counter. Then, looking through the front window, she said, "Your brothers are on the end of the dock."

"I ought to find out what they're up to. We don't see each other much since we moved out of our parents' house."

I wandered down the long dock, remembering when we would lie on our bellies and look through the cracks to watch the cow leeches. Once, Patrick caught a bunch and put them in my bed one night. I should have killed him right then.

"What's up?" I asked, when I got where Patrick dangled his feet off the edge.

"We're talking about the dead guy," George said. "Who do you think killed him?"

"How should I know?" I replied.

"I heard the cop say the wound looked like it was made with a fillet knife. The killer stuck it under his sternum and up into his left ventricle." Patrick is applying to medical school, and likes to talk about anatomy.

"Maybe we should try to find the murder weapon," George said.

"Don't you think the murderer would have thrown it into the lake?" Patrick replied.

"That's what we should have done with the hatchet that year,"

George said. "Remember the time we chopped down one of Bucky's trees, then got scared and buried the hatchet in the sand under the volleyball net?"

We sat quietly for a while, watching the loons play Duck and Cover. The sky was the blue you only see when you get far away from the Twin Cities, and the sun beat down on our thighs. It was one of those perfect afternoons I dig out of my memory bank in March when I'm sick of winter and can't get warm.

"Beat you to the buoy," I said, then dove in. George won, and crowed about it all afternoon.

The sun had passed its apex and the wind had died down when Bucky came by with the speed boat. "Wanna ski?" he asked.

Bucky taught all the kids at the resort how to ski. He would toss us the tow rope, then instruct us to tuck the skis under our bottoms. "Let the boat pull you up," he would say. "You can do it!"

He doesn't have to say that anymore. I've always been small, so it's easy for me to get up on one ski. I just pop out of the water. Because I'm the oldest, I was the first to learn to ski. I took pride in giving my brothers pointers. To this day, the smell of gasoline brings back the memory of those glorious afternoons, hanging on the tow rope while skimming across the water. I hope some day I can come here and teach my children to water ski.

"We need to build a bonfire tonight," I said later, over the hamburgers we'd grilled for dinner on the Weber in front of our cabin.

By midnight the fire was ablaze and the beer was gone. As usual, my brothers put away far more than I.

"You're an easy drunk," Patrick said to me.

"I'll put the fire out if you guys want to go to bed," I said, ignoring his comment.

After they had stumbled to our cabin, I filled the empty milk jug from the lake, and poured it on the fire. As the steam rose with a hiss, I slipped away.

Trying to walk as softly as the deer, I picked up a stick and headed for the volleyball court, where I dug up the knife. I took a rock and quietly as I could, nicked dings in the blade, so the pattern would be different from the one in the developer's chest. Then I stole behind the lodge and returned the knife to the fish-cleaning shed. Only the trees saw me.

"Nobody's going to buy this resort and turn it into a "North Woods gated community," I vowed, as I snuck back to our cabin and crawled into bed.